The Fifth Notch

Five men, five murderers, had destroyed his family and almost crippled him, but already Marshal Swan had brought four to justice. There were four notches on his gun and with just one more to go he rode for Highville, there to end his quest.

All he had to do was to find William Smith and call him out. But it didn't work out that way. Jack Swan found there was something even more important to him than vengeance – and an opponent no less deadly than himself.

A thrilling epic of the High Plains which recaptures the spirit of the Old West.

The Fifth Notch

MIKE STALL

A Black Horse Western

ROBERT HALE · LONDON

© Mike Stall 2002
First published in Great Britain 2002

ISBN 0 7090 7050 0

Robert Hale Limited
Clerkenwell House
Clerkenwell Green
London EC1R 0HT

Typeset by
Derek Doyle & Associates, Liverpool.
Printed and bound in Great Britain by
Antony Rowe Limited, Wiltshire

Contents

PROLOGUE

Missouri, 1867

Crump! A bullet smashed into the heavy shutters, but they held. The bullet probably came from a sixgun fired at some distance. The .50 calibres from the Sharps rifles came right through, which was why they were all kneeling. Ma with little Alice under the table, his brother Arthur and Pa firing back through the holes left at the bottom of the shutters for that very purpose. Pa had a Henry carbine and Arthur one of the two sixguns. Jack had wanted to shoot back himself but Arthur had told him to load so he always had a ready gun. Jack didn't like it but he could see it made sense.

'Jack!'

Jack put a loaded gun into Arthur's hand, took the hot Colt and started reloading. There wasn't much light, only the glow of the banked fire; they'd put out all the oil-lamps.

Crack! Crack! That was Pa firing with the repeating carbine. Was there a scream outside? It was hard to tell. Maybe just shouting. The fighting had been going on for half an hour and nobody had been hurt inside the house. Maybe nobody had been hurt outside either.

There were no answering shots. They all noticed.

'Please God they've gone,' Ma said softly.

'Don't you worry, Anne,' Pa said.

But she might just be right. They'd not fired for two, maybe three minutes. Maybe.... Jack forced himself to concentrate on loading the Colt. He was very afraid and almost as afraid to show it. Arthur didn't; he never did; and Pa was Pa. He glanced at his mother holding the little girl to her. Alice was weeping but Ma wasn't.

Still no firing. They'd gone, he was sure of it! He wanted to shout it out but he was listening too hard.

When it came the noise was totally unexpected. It was from the roof. A clumping sound. Jack couldn't understand it. On the roof.... and then he did understand, and so did Arthur and Pa. They started firing upwards and Jack, aware suddenly of the gun in his hand, started firing

8

too. He'd never fired a handgun before and the force of the recoil surprised him, but he kept on until it was empty. And then he heard Arthur calling for a pistol, but it was already too late as the fire came boiling out of the hearth as if Hell had opened a door. And he was screaming and Arthur was screaming and....

Then the blast came, not large but the door blew in and he seemed to be alight all over as the air fed the coal-oil flames pouring from the hearth. He was nearest the door and just for a second the coolness of the night touched him ... was lost again ... but it served to remind him it was there and he started for it, holding his hands over his face. He fled out into the yard, where he tripped over something unexpected and found himself rolling on the ground. Besides the awful surprise there was pain now, terrible pain in his back, and he rolled over and over trying to quench the flames eating into him, not taking his hands from his face, so he only heard the voices.

'Hell, it's just a kid.'

'Let him burn.'

But he didn't think of the speakers then, only of the family he'd abandoned. Then the shooting restarted, but it was all from outside now, fired in through the blown-off door and more celebratory than necessary. He only wished somebody would think to shoot him....

One
THE ACCIDENT

Jack Swan nooned early, mostly to allow his horse to take advantage of a section of particularly lush grass. He brewed coffee for himself but abstained from beans in favour of cold, cooked bacon. He was only a day away from Highville and he could fill up there on steak and side vegetables.

Out of habit he took out his Colt; checking it had been a daily ritual for years. The fourth notch still stood out, bright compared to the other three. Just one more and it was over. He suddenly felt a strong desire to toss it aside, leave it to rust here by the trail. What good had it ever done him? But instead he slipped it back into its holster. To just give up would be like disavowing his life and heritage. That he could never do willingly.

But he might have to do it anyway. The trail was now very cold. Aside from the name –

William Smith! – he had just the vaguest of locations: 'around Highville way', and even that information was old. But that would be different from just giving up. Trails end, and not always where or how you want them to, but in a day or so he would be in Highville and then, one way or another, it would be over. He'd be free.

How would it feel? Like a weight lifted from his shoulders? Or would he just become another drifter? Well, the High Plains were full of drifters, saddletramps, cowhands between jobs, gamblers, thieves, murderers and plain damn fools. They mightn't be good company but at least it would be substantial company.

Except here and now he had none at all, just the distant mountains, the peaks lost in the mist; only the lower slopes were clear, grassed in the foreground and with some tree-cover as the eye neared the hazy horizon. He put the remains of the bacon back in his saddle-bag, took a swig of coffee and rolled himself a cigarette. This was good land, worth staying for, and a long, long way from Missouri and from all those cattle towns where he'd financed his search, taking jobs as town-tamer, marshal and just plain bounty hunter when he had to. He'd have no rep out here. Except he would, after he'd found Smith....

He poured the remains of the bad coffee into the embers and started out for his horse.

He'd been riding for an hour when he heard the noise coming from below, a cry of some sort. He edged his horse to the side of the trail, looked down. It was a cowhand on a small horse. He peered. There was some scrub down there obscuring things. Finally he saw it – a steer. The cowhand was rounding up strayed stock. He wasn't very good at it. The steer was also very reluctant to rejoin the herd. The slope made it hard work, too. Swan hadn't known there were any ranches this high but he wasn't surprised. He'd long since got over letting things surprise him. And it was none of his business anyway.

Suddenly the little cowpony lost its footing; probably it had stood on a rock. He watched for it to get back up on its feet but it didn't, and the rider didn't either.

It was still none of his business, he told himself. But without conviction. It was easy enough to die in these uplands after a fall.

He glanced at the trail ahead. It turned away

15

in the wrong direction. There was nothing for it but to leave the trail and go downslope.

He did so, holding his horse in check, letting it find its own footings but keeping it slow. That was the trick of riding, to let the horse do all of the work and most of the thinking. But not quite all. Otherwise you ended up like the rider below.

It took him a quarter of an hour to get down to the horse and rider. It would take him longer to get back up, he thought as he dismounted. The cowpony was still down, trapping the cowhand still. Of the steer there was no sign.

'You look like you could use some help,' Swan said.

'I could.'

The voice surprised him. It was light, almost a boy's voice. He walked up to the rider, looked into the face. It wasn't a man at all!

'I'm OK, mister,' she said. 'If you can just get Buster to stand. I've been trying, but....'

Swan turned his attention to the horse. There was something suspect about a cowpony that would make no effort to rise. His suspicion was soon confirmed.

'It's broken its right foreleg,' he said.

'Oh no!' the woman said. 'Can you ...'

16

Swan shook his head. 'There's only one thing for it.' He drew his gun, his right hand snaking across his body to where it lay, butt first, in its holster. 'I can't risk even trying to get it up or moving it. How bad are you hurt?'

'I don't think I'm hurt at all. Just trapped.'

The gun fired once and was back in its holster before the sound had died off. The horse slumped. It crossed Swan's mind that it had made no noise, not even a solitary neigh, as if it had known its fate, maybe.

'I'll pull it off you downslope,' he said, slipping a rope under the cowpony's saddle-girth before mounting. 'Just get a good grip on the grass so you don't come with it.'

'OK.'

He applied pressure carefully. The horse couldn't feel anything but the rider could. He didn't pull the horse off all the way, just until only half of the rider's calf was still penned. Then he dismounted again and released the foot by tugging on the saddle-bow. She pulled her leg free easily enough.

'Thanks,' she began, 'I'll be OK now.'

'Don't try to stand. Let's take a look at that leg.'

'It feels fine,' she said. Then: 'Maybe just a little numb.' But she hadn't moved it, Swan noted.

He knelt by her. 'Excuse me,' he said and probed the calf and knee. That she was wearing trousers – Swan rather disapproved of such in the general course of things – was a convenience. 'Does that hurt?'

'A bit,' she said, looking rather white-faced. 'Help me up.'

He did.

She gasped with pain. 'Is it broken?'

'Torn muscles, I think. Maybe just rolled. It'll hurt like blazes but you'll be OK. You'll be dancing again in a month.'

She smiled at that. 'I don't get to do much dancing normally.'

And Swan saw that underneath the pain and despite the desexing men's clothes she was quite a pretty girl. No older than her early twenties, he guessed. What the hell she was doing playing ranch hand he couldn't guess.

'I'll put you on my horse,' he said. 'And—'

'Try not to fall off again?'

He smiled. 'I'd strongly advise it, ma'am.'

She laughed, then: 'If you'll help, I'll—'

The Fifth Notch

'No. Now's not the time to be walking on that leg.' He picked her up and carried her over to his horse, lifting her aboard. 'How far are you from home?'

''A mile or so.'

'Good. I'll lead the horse. I'm sorry, but I'll have to leave your saddle.'

'Esposito can fetch it,' she said quickly.

'No doubt, and as we're into names, mine's Swan. Jack Swan.'

'I'm obliged, Mr Swan. My name's Emma Smythe and I've been slow thanking you for ...'

'Let's just get you home now, Miss Smythe,' Swan said. 'Hang on tight. It's going to hurt.'

It did. She was whey-faced after no more than a few yards but she didn't cry out.

'Hang on,' he said, 'and tell me when we need another direction but downwards.'

'To the right,' she said between clenched teeth.

'It won't be long,' he said, knowing that pain was its own eternity.

The going was hard. On a good horse it would have been risky but challenging – a good ride. Leading, avoiding risks, seeing her looking increasingly distressed as she bestrode the horse, Swan found it peculiarly painful.

At last he saw the ranch house. It was larger than he'd imagined: plank-walled with a shingled roof and behind it a log-cabin style barn and a fair-sized corral. But for all its unexpected size there was no one about. He turned to Emma but now she was almost fainting in the saddle. He led the horse directly to the front door, called out but didn't wait to lift her down from the saddle.

'The door's open,' she said.

He carried her within, through a large hall into a main room with a piano, upholstered chairs and a sofa. He put her down gently on that. He called out again and this time he got some response. A middle-aged Mexican woman rushed in from the back, took one look at Emma and let out an explosion of Spanish. Emma responded, rather weakly, in the same language.

He stepped back. His work was done.

'I'll leave you, ma'am,' he said, touching his hat and, recalling he was in a house, removing it as he edged out.

Outside he breathed a sigh of relief. He didn't like to be around sickness and pain. It was said that pain left no memory but it was only half true. He would always recall the feeling that went with it – the animal-like submission, the impotence, the rage.

He looked for his horse. He had neglected to hitch it to the rail but it had only walked over to the drinking-trough to the side of the house. He walked over towards it slowly. There was no reason not to let it drink its fill. The climb down had been tricky rather than exhausting. It hadn't worked up a sweat.

His horse had had enough by the time he got to it. He took hold of the reins, prepared to mount.

'Mister.'

Swan tensed. His hand moved across his body over to his Colt but something stopped him from drawing. Partly the voice, partly the circumstances. He turned, and saw a man standing outside the front door. Except it wasn't exactly a man, more a boy. Fifteen, sixteen … it was hard to say. He was tall, not too far short of six feet, but there was little meat on the bones as yet. He wasn't wearing a gun.

'Yeah?'

'You're not leaving, are you?'

'I was thinking of it.'

The boy hesitated, then: 'We'd like you to stay.

21

So we can tell you thanks.'

'Anybody would have done the same.'

'Round these parts, maybe not.' The boy walked over to him. 'The least we can do is feed your horse and invite you to dinner.'

Swan smiled, patted his horse with the hand that had hovered over the gun.

'Hear that girl, you've been invited to hay. I come second.'

The boy smiled. 'You know I didn't exactly mean that.'

'Maybe you should have. It was the horse who carried your ...' He paused.

'Sister.' The boy was close enough to offer his hand. 'I'm Wilson Smythe but folks just call me Wilse.'

'Jack Swan.'

'I've heard that name before.'

'I'm not from these parts,' Swan said.

'So what about dinner? Mamacita's a fine cook.'

Instinct told him to move on, but it would take him a couple of hours to get back to the trail and there'd hardly be time to set up camp before it was dark. A fed and rested horse, not to mention a warm meal inside himself, could do little harm.

And he liked the boy. He'd liked Emma. She hadn't whined or wept.

The delay was fatal. 'I'll tell Mamacita to set you a plate,' Wilse said and ran off.

'I'll take your horse, *señor*.'

Swan turned to see an old Mexican. From being deserted the ranch had suddenly become crowded. It was the way of things. But Swan realized he'd been given a second chance. He could say no now and ride off.

He was tempted.

'I call myself Esposito,' the old man said, taking the reins from him and leading the horse off in the direction of the stables. 'We are very grateful *señor*.'

Swan shook his head but only to the old man's retreating back. Apparently, against his better judgement, he was staying for dinner. And probably a bed too. Why had he let himself be pushed into it? He wasn't usually indecisive.

He walked over to the corral rail and leaned against it, took out the makings and rolled himself a cigarette. He laughed shortly to himself. Now the search was nearing its end he was getting like a leaf blowing in the wind. So be it. At least he'd landed in the vicinity of hot food and a soft bed. It could be worse. He lit the cigarette and drew on it, thinking of nothing much at all.

TWO
TARR

It wasn't exactly a pool, more a place where the stream went very wide and shallow over the rocks in the high valley, but the cattle weren't fussy about geographic terms so long as there was some rich herbage about. There were seven of them, strayed pp from the eastern side of the ranch. They were happy enough cropping so Swan and Wilse took the opportunity of resting their horses and, almost inevitably, took off their boots and bathed their feet in the cool mountain water.

It was three days since Swan had brought Emma back to the ranch. They'd all pressed him to stay and, almost despite himself, Swan had caved in. And as they were a hand short, he'd decided to earn his keep.

'Hell,' Wilse said, as if he used that word and much worse as a matter of course, which he didn't, 'my feet are cold. I reckon I'm near getting them frostbit.' He promptly extracted them from the water.

Swan smiled. He knew the kid was trying to impress him and appear grown up. His folks were dead save for his sister, and he was pretty much under her thumb. He wasn't even allowed to carry a gun. Maybe he was too young for a Colt but the ban extended even to a saddle-gun and that was an essential tool for a buckaroo. Maybe he was a kid, but he was doing a man's work and.... Swan stopped himself. It was plainly none of his business, after all.

'Don't you feel the cold?'

'I enjoy it,' Swan said. 'Heck, if it was deep enough I'd go in all the way.'

'It is over there. It's up to your shoulders – at least it would be if you sat down in it.'

'I think I just might. We've time, haven't we?'

Wilse glanced at the sun. 'Sure.' He didn't sound enthusiastic.

Swan stood up, laughing. 'Just me. You can stand guard.'

Wilse smiled.

Swan stripped down to his undervest and long johns and walked up the streambed to the place indicated. He sat down but it was way off his shoulders. He had to half lie to get the water to where his back was itching. Wilse had walked up alongside to talk to him.

'It looks cold,' he said.

'It sure is,' Swan said, luxuriating in the coldness. He always bathed in cold water, always had since.... 'You're sure you don't want to come in?'

Wilse laughed. 'I'd die of pneumonia. Or worse, survive, and Sis would chaff at me for ever over it.'

That was probably true. She was very protective. But why not? He was all she had.

'Hey, Jack, will you teach me how to shoot? It's too far from the ranch for them to hear and ...' Wilse broke off.

'Sorry, Wilse, but we'd only spook the cattle.' Swan felt suddenly guilty. It was a modest enough request. Emma was unreasonable with the kid but somehow he didn't want to risk it. He pushed it out of his mind. The cold was seeping into his bones and he was thoroughly enjoying it. Maybe too much. He stood up. 'There's a cloth, an undervest and a spare pair of long johns in my saddlebag. If you'd get them for me ...'

'Surely.'

Swan walked to the side now, anxious to get

dry. The pleasure was in the coldness, not in clamminess. Wilse hurried back.

'Thanks.'

Then Wilse just stood there.

Swan laughed. 'Hell, give me some privacy.'

'Sorry.' The boy turned about.

He'd been like that since Swan had arrived, running at his heels like a puppy, he'd thought as he towelled himself dry.

It was understandable. No father, no brother and he hadn't even been much in school. It was too far and besides, Emma had had a normal school education and now had a desire to teach. He pulled on his long johns – plain ones, not the pink ones so many buckaroos favoured. He was pulling on his undervest when the kid turned to him and said:

'There's somebody coming ...' He stopped, seeing the scars on Swan's back. Swan pulled down the vest quickly.

'Who and where?'

Wilse just looked at him.

'I was in a fire once,' Swan said shortly, walking back to where he'd left his clothes. 'Now, where ...' But he could see them himself now, several hundred yards off, coming up the way they themselves had come. Three of them, wranglers by the look of it. He dressed quickly, pulling on his boots with his feet still wet. Then he strapped on his gunbelt. That felt much better. He didn't fancy the idea of meeting strangers out on the range naked.

'Let's get mounted,' he said to Wilse.

'They're only Bar X men,' Wilse said.

Swan mounted up. 'So these are just local buckaroos and you've no dispute with them?'

'Sometimes, mostly at round-up, but not lately.'

Everybody argued about unbranded steers at round-up. It normally meant nothing.

'How did you—' Wilse began.

'Stay behind me,' Swan said. He had no real reason for it; the wranglers weren't riding at a gallop; their progress was even leisurely, but out in the wilderness he'd learnt it was wise to be careful.

'Hi, fella,' the first of the wranglers said as they drew up. He was a tall man on a not very tall horse, his black hair flowing out from under a nondescript hat. He also needed a shave. But he kept his hands on the reins, well away from the gun on his right hip. 'And it's the Smythe boy too. A bit out of your territory.'

'Maybe,' Swan said. 'We're collecting strays. Have a look at 'em if you like. They're all branded.'

'I'll take your word for that,' the man said. 'But they're still on Bar X land.'

'It's government range,' Wilse said from behind him.

'Out of the mouths of babes and sucklings!' The man laughed, showing a full set of perfect, shiny white teeth. 'Except we reckon otherwise.'

'I'm still taking them back to the Smythe ranch,' Swan said, quite softly.

'You take a lot on yourself, mister. You work for the Smythes?'

'Passing through. But I've eaten their bread and slept under their roof as a guest and that involves certain responsibilities.'

'You sound like a lawyer.'

'I'm not,' Swan said.

One of the other two riders moved his horse nearer the first, trying to whisper something to him. But the top hand was on his mettle.

'Say whatever it is out loud, Kelsey. We've no secrets from our friends.'

'You asked, Tarr. It's just that I've seen this fella before.'

'And is it a secret where that was?'

'In Hadleytown. He was marshal there.'

Tarr's eyes fixed on Swan. 'So you're *the* Jack Swan Never went to Hadleytown myself but I heard tell of it a whole lot.'

'I've marshalled in other towns.'

'And done some bounty hunting too, I heard.'

'What's it to you?'

Tarr smiled again, rather more tightly. 'Just interest, Mr Swan, just interest. We don't expect to meet people out here and never anybody famous.'

'We're taking the cattle now,' Swan said. 'Any objections?'

Tarr wanted to object, he could see. He wasn't a man to back down, least of all with two of his underlings to witness the fact. But he was a buckaroo, a cowboy, no more.

'Well, as a concession to our famous guest, and as the cattle are all branded, I don't reckon we object.'

Swan half smiled. Tarr had just turned the back-down into a concession and insisted on the 'we' rather than the 'I' to save face. Except he wasn't going to get away with it that easily.

'You ride down first. I don't want you spooking the cattle.'

The cattle wouldn't be spooked by three experienced wranglers. They all knew that. And for all he'd spoken softly Swan hadn't even put in a 'will you'. It had been a straight order.

Tarr took it. He didn't like it but he'd already decided to back down, and for good reason. He said not a further word but turned his horse and set off down. The other two followed him.

Swan watched them for a while, then became aware that Wilse's horse was beside his.

'You made Tarr eat crow!' said the kid, evidently happy about it.

Swan suddenly wasn't. Maybe Tarr had been in the right. He didn't know. He hadn't even been angry with the man. In his line of work you didn't last long if you got angry. Except, he recalled, he wasn't in that line of work at this precise moment. So why had he gone on the prod? Maybe because he'd been careless enough to let someone see his deformed back.

'Kelsey said you were a marshal,' Wilse said. He paused as if trying to recall something. Then: 'You're Fighting Jack Swan! You were in that shoot-out with Choctaw Bill Sullen! And—'

'Let's get the cattle back,' Swan said shortly. 'It's getting late.'

*

It should have been a pleasant evening. Emma was seated in a chair when they returned; she'd walked to the dinner-table with a stick. She was wearing a green dress which Wilse casually referred to as her 'town dress' and received a very cutting look for it, not that he noticed. He was busting to tell of the confrontation in the high valley. Emma kept cutting him off; she didn't want to talk shop.

The table was beautifully set with their best porcelain and silver as if to assert that they – specifically, she – hadn't forgotten totally about culture and civilization out here in the wilderness. There was even a bottle of Spanish-style wine, a touch too syrupy for Swan's taste though he avoided saying so. Wilse was far too delighted to be allowed a glass to even think of criticizing it. The food was good if you liked Mexican cuisine which Swan did, more or less, though he preferred coffee and a steak. And for afterwards there were cigars, a box of them, presumably her late father's. Swan politely declined, afraid the cigars would   disintegrate if he touched them, which they might well have done, embarrassing

35

her. The last thing he wanted.

It was Wilse who broke through the constraints.

'We met Tarr in the mountains,' he said.

Swan let him tell it. He did it pretty accurately too, and didn't mention the burns on Swan's back, which he was grateful for.

'I don't suppose there would really have been any trouble,' she said. 'After all—'

'But there would. Tarr was really on the prod. He seemed annoyed that Jack was staying with us' – a very pointed look was wasted on the boy – 'but Kelsey knew Jack – Fighting Jack Swan, the marshal.'

For a brief moment he saw the pain in her face. The leg had to be agonizing still but she'd kept the pain under control. Her surprise let it peep through for a moment – and then the control was back, iron-hard now. She looked at Swan as if for the first time. Obviously she'd heard of him. His rep varied in different regions but pretty clearly the version she'd heard hadn't pleased her.

'I'd like to be a marshal too someday—' Wilse began.

Swan reacted quickly to forestall a response from Emma. 'No, you wouldn't. It's a pretty poor life. I've thrown it in myself.'

If anything, her face hardened further. 'Wilse, you've work to do tomorrow. I think you'd best get to bed.'

'But—'

'You've drunk wine too. You're not used to it.'

'Yes, ma'am,' he said, a little rebelliously but without any real rebellion. He stood up, smiled, then: 'Goodnight, Sis. Goodnight, Jack.'

'He's good boy,' Swan said when he'd gone.

'He is,' she said. 'I want him to stay that way.'

He won't: he's turning into a man. The words formed in Swan's mind but he didn't voice them. He could see from her face now what was coming – an invitation to leave.

But she said nothing. He considered striking first, something on the lines of: *I reckon I'll be moving on tomorrow, now you're back on your feet*. But he said nothing.

'I worry about him,' she admitted suddenly.

Swan nodded. 'There's one thing, I'd have a care with the Bar X. Tarr was in an ugly mood.' He certainly had been when he left but Swan fancied he had been when he arrived too. 'On the prod' was as good a way as any of describing it.

'I don't think you need worry. Mr Rivers owns

the Bar X and we get on well enough.'

No doubt they did. He was the stranger here and however he read Tarr she was going to interpret it as somewhat jaundiced. He was a killer with a badge. And maybe she wasn't too far out at that. He could hardly say: *I had my reasons ... I'm not like that really.* Even if he felt like apologizing for the life he'd led, which he didn't. No, for all he hadn't been asked, it would soon be time to be moving on. An idyll was over. That's what happened with idylls. All the same, he found himself saying:

'I can stay on a few more days to help out around the ranch, if you need me.'

She smiled. 'Thank you.' Then: 'I'll say goodnight now, Jack.' She got to her feet with difficulty and paused a second, as if considering whether to use the stick. She didn't. Swan looked at her in the lamplight, strained and tired, in an antique green dress that had probably been her mother's, and decided she was the loveliest girl he had ever seen. And then she was gone, limping off to her room.

He reached over the dirty dishes – this was probably the first time the dinner porcelain had been left unwashed overnight in this house –

and took one of the cigars. It didn't disintegrate, though it did have a crumbly feel to it, and lit it from the oil-lamp.

It was on the dry side but very smokeable none the less.

A few more days. Days that could be made to stretch out into weeks, months, years. Emma obviously hadn't been best pleased to discover something of his past but she'd said nothing. And it wasn't exactly a shameful past. He'd kept on the right side of the law, more or less. It could be forgotten.

Except, had he the right to forget? All those years ago he'd made himself a promise. He'd kept it till now. Could he forget it?

What did he have? The commonest of names and a very general location. He could search for years and find nothing. Was that it – he was to have nothing for himself?

He'd stay a few more days at least.

He was awake well before dawn and with no likelihood of getting back to sleep. He went out into the half-light, took out the makings, put them back. It wasn't wise to get used to places ...

and people. He had only been here a few days but the place already felt utterly familiar. And he'd never met a woman he admired as he did Emma.

He had a decision to make. He put his hand on the butt of his gun that had become part of his clothing. Too much so, maybe. And yet....

He walked over to the stables. He might as well be employed as not. It was half a decision. and he realized it. Hell, she might still ask him to leave. But he knew she wouldn't.

The horses didn't welcome his early intrusion or even pay him any attention. The light was still poor and they reckoned it was still night. Maybe they were right. He let them be and looked around. He was pretty good at searching but he wasn't looking for anything, just passing time. He felt relieved and guilty for the decision that was firming in his mind. He'd stay, given any encouragement.

He noticed the old saddle as the light brightened and suddenly flooded in through the open door, set easterly for that purpose. A clever touch, that. Whoever had built this had had sense. He walked over to the saddle, intrigued. It had been cleaned but not used in an age. One of Emma's old saddles? Or maybe one of her father's, left here as some kind of memorial?

That seemed the likeliest prospect. He knew that her father had died some years back of fever but that was all. Out of curiosity he examined the saddle, its leather cracking from lack of use. Finally he noticed the branded name: Wm. Smith.

He caught his breath. It was indeed a common enough name, and people did change it to Smythe to avoid its very commonness. But not out here in the wilds. Here they did it for a different reason – to hide. He'd check it out but he already knew. He'd never put that fifth notch on his gun. Fever had beaten him to it.

He walked quickly out into the burgeoning light. Within moments of deciding to abandon his crusade he had been given proof of its complete success. He ought to be happy, relieved. But he felt nothing of the sort. Worse, his feelings for Emma – and his liking for Wilse – hadn't changed in the slightest. He felt that they ought to have, that he should see them in a darker light, but he didn't. God might punish unto the fourth generation but he was just a man with a list. An old list. A finished list.

He glanced around the ranch. Never get

attached to people and places. The thought mocked him, for there was no reason he shouldn't, now. His task was accomplished. But there was no staying, not now, not ever. After a moment he went back inside to saddle his horse.

'He's gone,' Wilse said, running into the kitchen.

'Are you sure?' Emma asked.

Wilse nodded. 'His horse is gone. He's packed up his things and left.' He paused. 'Do you think it was something I said?'

Emma shook her head. 'No, he was just passing through.'

But Wilse had never seen his sister look so forlorn.

Three
THE TOWN

Highville was a single street lost on the high prairie. Technically it had many streets but they were just names given to the gaps between the buildings that made up Main Street. There were three saloons, a Congregationalist chapel, a tiny jailhouse, a general store, a milliner's – which was really an adjunct to the dry-goods store – and that was about it. The owners of the stores lived above them, doing away with need for private houses. There was no town hall. But there would be a mayor and a town council, Swan knew. And maybe both would be good. There was no way of telling from appearances. If Highville were still here and thriving in ten years, they were good; if not, it would just add to the regiment of ghost towns that dotted the High Plains.

Swan took his weary horse to the livery stable when he rode in as the afternoon was giving way to evening. It was on the northern edge of town with a large sign that said SHAW'S STABLES. Swan smiled at the power of alliteration and led his horse into the building. An oldster, toting a sixgun on his hip but in a fastened-down flap-holster, approached him.

'Don't say it,' Shaw said.

'Say what?'

'Why wear it if you can't get to it? And the like.'

So they were talking about the gun. 'I never said anything.'

'Not surprising with a cross-over rig like yours. I wore this gun everyday for years 'cos of the Indians. Now they're all on reservations or in Florida but the habit stays with you. You'll be Swan.'

'Yeah,' Swan said, unsurprised by the man and his unconventional greeting. You didn't get old on the Frontier by being conventional. This was a tough, smart old bird. Who also knew his name.

'I suppose the Bar X boys were in one of the saloons last night.'

'Tarr was,' Shaw said, 'and a couple of his yes men.' He spat. 'They damn near ask his permission to spit.' He paused. 'He reckons you're a hired gun for the Smythes.'

'Just passing through.'

'That's transient rate then,' the oldster said, 'seventy-five cents a day or five bucks if you compound for the week.'

'Why not?' Swan said, though why he should want to spend a week in this back-of-beyond hole he didn't know.

'You can change your mind if you want to,' Shaw said, taking the reins. 'The Grafton is the best hotel. It's also a saloon. Or you can sleep here, just so long as you don't eat hay.' He cackled suddenly at that little joke and started to lead the horse off.

'One thing, Mr Shaw,' Swan said to the departing back of the oldster, 'how can anybody be sure you've really got a dogleg in that holster? You might have a pint of bourbon in there instead.'

The oldster turned. 'Maybe I could at that. Nobody else ever thought of that.' He smiled, suddenly revealing surprisingly good teeth. 'I reckon I could get to like you. So be careful of young Williams.'

'Never heard of him.'

'No reason you should. He's a drifter, been helping out round town these last few weeks. After a job with the Bar X, I reckon. Last night

47

he saw a way. Talked big. Said he'd kill you.'
Shaw turned and got on with business.

'I'm obliged,' Swan said and did likewise.

Swan went straight to the jailhouse. He was
surprised by the notice on the door:

ABE CAMERON
DEP SHERIFF

He'd expected a city marshal's office, not a tenta-
cle of the county sheriff. He went inside.

Abe Cameron was asleep with his feet on the
desk. The cell door to his right was open, the
keys in the lock. Swan glanced around taking in
the details with a practised eye. There were only
three guns visible: a duty Colt on the desk itself
and two shotguns on a wall rack. They weren't
locked up in any way. There were a couple of
ancient dodgers – wanted posters – thumbtacked
to the wall. And that was it. Except for the
deputy himself who looked even older than Shaw
at the livery stable.

'Deputy.'

'Eh, what's that?' Cameron said, opening a
rheumy eye to look up at his visitor.

'Sorry to wake you, Deputy, but I'm Swan.'

Cameron swung his leg from the desk, properly waking up now. 'Heard about you, Marshal.' He shook his head, not in negation but as if to throw off the last tentacles of sleep. 'I'd offer you a chair but there ain't one. No room.'

That was true enough. It was the smallest peace office Swan had yet seen.

'Sit on the desk if you care to.'

'I've been riding.'

'Yeah. Now, how can I help.'

'Two things. I thought I'd better introduce myself, professional courtesy ...'

'Yeah, much appreciated.'

'And I hear a certain Williams is threatening to kill me. I thought I'd better discuss the matter with you.'

'Why?' the oldster asked, looking at him sharply.

Swan pointed to the badge the deputy was wearing.

'Hell, I just hand out tax notices and get paid thirty dollars a month for it, accommodation found.' He gestured towards the cell. 'I'm no gunfighter and the sheriff knows it. Besides, you don't need to worry about the likes of Williams.

Do what you want with him. I heard him threaten you.'

'Thanks.'

'You staying around?'

'A few days.'

'Watch out for the Bar X boys. Not that I reckon 'em much. More talk than shooting – but who the hell am I to talk?'

There was nothing to say to that. The old man had been honest with him, brutally honest about himself. Swan did him the courtesy of a polite lie.

'I'm obliged,' he said, and left.

The 'Grafton' had three men at the bar and none of them was Williams. Two of them were the wrong age and the third, though he was wearing a Colt, had none of the tenseness of the killer or would-be killer about him. Swan knew: it was knowing such things that had kept him alive.

'Whiskey?'

'A beer,' Swan told the barkeep, another oldish man. He was about to ask for a room but something stopped him. He had never been here before and neither Shaw nor Cameron were exactly gossips. Anonymity preserved a little longer might prove very useful.

The beer arrived in a tall glass, too much of it head. He drank anyway, thirsty from the trail. But not all of it. At this time of day you drew less attention to yourself by nursing a drink. He reached for the makings, thought better of it and bought himself a nickel cigar from the barkeep who lit it for him. It wasn't great but it was a touch fresher than the one he had smoked the night before at the Smythes. He drew on it, relaxing, and had an idea.

'Cards,' he said to the barkeep.

'A new pack?'

'House cards are good enough.'

A dog-eared set was put into his hand and he walked over to the corner table, still carrying the remains of his beer in the heavy glass. He sat down and dealt out two poker hands, face down. After a moment he turned one up. Two pairs. He left the other hand face down still. He leaned back against the wall, drew on his cigar and waited, his mind drawn back to the few days he'd spent at the Smythe ranch before his discovery had truly shattered the idyll. He'd played cards with Wilse and Emma, sat beside her bed – poker for matchsticks. He smiled at the memory. She'd never have made her living as a professional gambler, being too fond of upping the ante on a pair or even a high. If the matches hadn't been handed back at the end of the game he'd have been the lucifer king of the Smythe ranch. And he didn't count himself as an exceptional gambler. He could hold his own if the cards were dealt from the top, and they usually were in his presence, but that was all.

But Emma wouldn't have thought of making money in that way. She'd spent a year away from home in the state capital at the Normal School for Teachers, before her parents died, and she had a rather schoolmarmish attitude to gambling. And drinking. And guns.

What the hell am I doing thinking about her? Why am I hanging about this God forsaken place? It was pointless. The past lay between them like stone and it would be even worse if he killed this Williams....

He was on his third glass of beer and second cigar when Williams entered. He couldn't have advertised his presence better with a sign; the gun was low-slung on his right hip, tied off, and it shone as if continually polished, which it would be. The clothes were travel-stained but Kansas City-made, the jacket too short, the trousers too tight and short, and the Stetson too large. He was a young man trying to look older and more dangerous than he was, but he was already dangerous enough. He'd be fast on the draw, maybe faster than himself, but that was no real worry. Unless he missed his bet Williams had never drawn on anybody yet, let alone killed anyone.

But that wouldn't last. And if he were unlucky enough to try it out with a pro, not a drunken cowboy, he'd get himself killed. Swan had killed a few like him already. Men on the prod, after a rep and as dangerous as wolves. Except he was a wolfer.

'Fancy a game?' Swan called out. Williams turned, looked him over. Swan had taken off his gunbelt, set it between himself and the wall so its crossover style was impossible to see. Unless the kid knew him by sight he was just another fellow met in a saloon playing cards.

Williams downed his first whiskey. 'Hit me again.' The barkeep obliged and then went off to light the lamps outside. It was getting darker. He'd lit the interior ones a quarter of an hour before. Williams picked up his glass and walked over, hindered a little by his large rowel spurs.

'Why not?'

'Stud?'

'Why not?' Williams said, sitting down. He looked about nineteen with spotty cheeks and dark, piercing eyes. Just a wild kid.

'Dime a raise, three dollar limit.'

'You're no hustler,' the kid said, smiling.

But that was just the way a hustler would take him, start low and suck him in. Though a smart hustler would avoid him like the plague; he'd be a bad player but also a very bad loser.

'You Williams?' Swan said, putting a handful of dimes on the table.

'How did you know?'

'Seen you around.' There was something flattering about that and Williams didn't query it. He wanted to be seen around – *the* Fred Williams.

Swan finished off his beer and waited as Williams brought out nickels and dimes. He was setting them down on the table when Swan brought down the heavy glass on his hand, aiming for the right forefinger.

Williams screamed like a woman, kicked back away from the table and fell on the floor, grasping his right hand with his left. He didn't go for his gun.

54

'You bastard!'

Swan stood up. 'My name's Swan. I heard you wanted to kill me.'

'I'd've called you out!'

'Maybe. Or backshot me.' Swan walked over, took hold of the kid's right forearm and prised off the protective left hand. The finger was already beginning to swell.

'Waggle it,' Swan commanded.

Too shocked to do otherwise, Williams obliged.

'Not broken, though there could be a hairline fracture. It'll come up like a balloon. It'll hurt like hell too. But in a fortnight it'll be as good as new.'

'I'll kill you!'

'You were going to anyway. Or so you said. But you didn't even know me. Face it, kid, you're not mean enough for this game. If you want a man dead, you kill him. You don't threaten him.' Swan took him by the shoulders, lifted him easily to his feet, relieving him of his Colt in the process. 'I'll leave this with the barkeep. Now go see to that finger.'

'I'll—'

'I told you about threats. Look at you, no gun and unable to shoot one if you had. I've just saved your life, kid. Keep it safe. Get on your horse and ride. Try your hand as a buckaroo but not as a killer. You don't rate, and lucky for you too.'

'I'll get the law on you.'

'I've already seen the deputy,' Swan said reasonably. 'You'd threatened my life.'

Impotent with pain and rage Williams looked around the saloon as if hoping the other patrons, still few in number, would stand by him. They were all smiling. He looked back at Swan, who wasn't. His expression was worse – almost pitying. Williams turned and left, still impeded by the rowel spurs.

Swan handed the Colt to the barkeep. 'Hold it for him.'

'I don't reckon he'll be back.'

Swan shrugged.

'Have a whiskey on the house,' the barkeep said. 'What's your name, anyway?'

Swan told him.

'And the bottle too! Hell, I'm glad I was here to see that.' The other patrons were laughing now; a little bit of history had been made and they'd been present. He knew that if he stayed he'd not need to buy a drink all evening. He had what Williams had craved: he was the hero.

'Have you got a room?' he asked the barkeep.

'First floor on your right. The keys are in the locks.'

'Fine,' Swan said, downing his whiskey and heading for the stairs. He didn't feel like celebrating what had been a deceptive and brutal act. Usually he would have ridden on or killed the guy. He just hadn't wanted to kill here. Unless you were wearing a star you couldn't kill and stay on, however justified it was.

The celebration went on quite a while. It stopped him sleeping and he regretted not buying some cigars, but he didn't want to go down. He sat by the window and looked out at the stars over the high prairie: cold lights, colder than snow in the sierras.

Cattle were unutterably stupid creatures, Wilse thought, riding to the left of his little herd to bring in the stragglers. But there was no malice in the thought; he liked them, liked working with them, and took pleasure in moving them around as he was doing today to take advantage of the better grass. Besides, their stupidity did have its good side; if they'd been as quick and as clever as bobcats who could have handled them?

He fancied there were new stragglers on the mountain beside the pool but he studiously avoided that area at Emma's insistence. She didn't want any trouble with the Bar X. He hadn't argued. Standing up to Tarr was fine when Swan was there but he was two days gone and Wilse was out here on his own. Maybe it was better to keep on indisputable Smythe range. Even if he was near the edge of it. That little bunch of trees, bent by the winds, marked the boundary and he was still a hundred yards off it.

A bunch of cows started edging out again 'Dammed idiots,' he said, using words he would not risk at home, and rode out to edge them back in. Why had Jack ridden off like that without a word? He'd asked Emma again but gotten nothing from her. Her answer amounted to; *he just did*. He was nearly sixteen and no longer believed people 'just' did anything but he also knew you couldn't argue with women and expect to win. They had their own set of rules and even if you seemed to be winning by them they countered by suddenly changing them.

He smiled. Sis wasn't so bad really. She'd kept the ranch together working as hard as any man and harder. It couldn't have been easy coming back from the state capital with a teacher's certificate and your life mapped out and have to run a ranch and raise a kid. Except he wasn't a kid any more. Hell, with her hurt – though she was getting better by the day – he'd been running things, more or less, and making a damn' fine job of it.

'Get on with you!' he shouted at a recalcitrant cow and it duly obliged though he knew it was the presence of himself and his practised cowpony that did the trick. Cows were indifferent to being shouted at. Just another hour, he thought....

And then he saw them, the same three. They'd come out of the trees. In fact they were fifty yards off and on Smythe range but he quickly decided not to make anything of it. In fact, it might be better to put distance between them and himself. He started to edge the herd away from them.

But they were riding over. Maybe just to offer a hand. Tarr wasn't all that bad. A few years back when he'd first come to the Bar X he'd come over Sundays. Mamacita had said he was trying to 'spark' Sis. He hadn't understood it quite at the time but he did now. But Sis hadn't been interested. Not at all.

They were up to him now riding just ahead. Then Tarr turned his horse and stopped directly in front of him. Wilse eased back on the reins.

'Hey mister—'

'Don't "hey" me, boy. Kelsey, check the herd. I want to know if there are any Bar X cows here.'

'These are all Smythe cattle,' Wilse said. 'Anyway, you're on Smythe land.'

'You're telling me where I am, boy? Where I can ride?' He wasn't shouting, not even raising his voice much but there was something in his tone that made the hairs on the back of Wilse's neck rise.

'There's a couple of Bar X cows here, Tarr,' Kelsey said without even getting off his horse.

'That's a lie!'

'You're going to let a kid call you a liar, Kelsey?'

'Hell no.'

Suddenly Wilse felt the lariat snaking over his head. The line tightened about his arms and at a nod from Tarr he was jerked from his horse. He landed heavily but not all the breath was knocked out of him.

'You can't do this ...' he began but a jerk of rope flattened him to the ground.

60

'We let rustlers talk to us like that?' Tarr said, mockingly now. 'Let's show him how we handle cattle thieves out here.'

Wilse suddenly found himself being pulled behind Kelsey's horse through the grass, slowly at first, then the walk became a canter and almost a gallop. The ground banged at him. He tried to keep his head up but the rope twisted and he felt like a rag doll. When they finally stopped there was a cut on his head from a rock and blood was trickling into his eyes. The rope was like an iron band round him, cutting agonizingly into his pinned arms.

'He hasn't got so much to say for himself now,' Tarr said.

Wilse looked up at him, trying to free his arms from the rope but the knot had tightened too much. He tried to speak but the words froze in his throat.

'You ain't on Smythe land now, boy,' Tarr said dismounting. 'And you won't be on Bar X land long, either.'

Wilse watched him take the rope from his saddle, approach him. Incredibly, he was fashioning a noose, just a simple slip-noose, nothing fancy with thirteen turns, but his intentions were clear. And unbelievable.

'He's just a kid, ' Kelsey said.

'You told me they were Bar X stock. Going back on that?'

'No, Tarr.'

Wilse tried to shy away from Tarr but a kick in the ribs stilled him. Tarr knelt to put the noose around his neck.

'Ain't got your pal the gunman with you now, have you, kid?' he taunted, tightening the noose until it bit but not too hard. Then he walked back to his horse, remounted, still holding the end of the rope.

'I don't think—' the third rider began.

'Right. I do the thinking here,' Tarr said viciously. 'If he's old enough to steal cattle, he's old enough to hang.'

Wilse still didn't believe it could be happening to him. Not even when he saw they were by the trees, saw Tarr throw the lariat's end over one of the higher branches and catch it again.

'I'll fetch his horse,' Kelsey said.

'Hell, we don't need to,' Tarr said, jerked Wilse to his feet.

The pain was bad but Wilse kept standing somehow. They were playing a game with him, a nasty cruel game but eventually they'd stop, cut him free and ride off.

'Let's see if the kid can dance,' he heard Tarr say and suddenly the rope around his neck was biting again and he was in the air. He kicked out wildly, searching for ground that wasn't there. And then he was swinging. He could see Tarr leaning from his saddle to tie off to the tree just before the world went red. This wasn't happening, he told himself: he was having a nightmare. But the pain was real – a band of fire around his neck.

Oddly, he could breathe if he gasped but he couldn't stop himself kicking and every time he did so the noose tightened a little. His face felt like it was about to explode; he disgraced himself like a child and he wanted to weep like a child but he couldn't. He swung and swung and the agony was beyond bearing but unconsciousness took a long time coming.

The last thing Wilse heard was Tarr laughing.

Four
THE MARSHAL

'Something's biting,' Swan said and something was. It turned out to be a catfish, somewhat on the smallish side. Swan hauled it in and gaffed it but didn't cast out again. Together with the two he'd caught previously and Cameron's three it made a sufficiency. Cameron already had two in the pan he'd brought, frying noisily in hot grease. They smelt good.

'The Indians had a way with fish,' Cameron said. 'They kinda cooked them in the ashes of the fire, wrapped in clay if they'd the time. Mighty good.'

'Are there many left?'

'Catfish or Indians?' Cameron laughed, with just a touch of the cackle in it that came inevitably with age. 'Hell, I reckon the catfish did better.' He paused. 'When I was your age a man took his rifle with him everywhere and none of your fancy Winchesters that shoot from here to

Sunday. Hell, some were even flintlocks.'

'Even the Indians?'

'Damn it, they didn't have no rifles then. I'd be dead if they had. Just bows and spears.'

'Sounds unpleasant,' Swan said, more interested in the catfish frying noisily over the creekside fire.

'Arrows ain't no fun but it's pretty hard to kill a man with an arrow, Old Mo' Johnson got shot straight through the face. He was a hootin' and a hollerin' and it went in one cheek and out the other like a bridle, so to speak. He tried to bite down on it, couldn't. Had to break it off and pull it through.'

'And?'

'He'd two little puckered scars on his cheeks for the rest of his life. Didn't harm him none. The two Indians after him didn't fare so well. An arrow through the mouth don't stop a man shooting and he used a fifty calibre. You don't pull those slugs out so easy.'

'Hard days,' Swan said.

'Were they really? Thinking back, maybe. But I was young then. Hell of a thing to be young, Swan. Make sure you appreciate it.'

Swan didn't feel all that young or much appreciative of anything. He'd been hanging around town to no purpose for several days. Coming out with the deputy to catch fish in the creek like a couple of boys truanting from school was the most useful thing he'd done. It was time to be moving on.

'Take one. They're done,' Cameron said, offering the pan.

Swan did, using the knife to lift it from the pan and hold it a space to let it cool. Cameron's gnarled fingers were insulation enough for his catfish and with the other hand he was slapping the remaining catfish into the hot grease.

Swan started on the fish. It was good and all the better for being their own catch, caught and eaten in the open air.

'I reckon you'll be moving on soon,' Cameron said. It was nearly a question.

'Why?' Swan asked through a mouthful of hot catfish.

'When a young fellow like you hangs about, it's usually for a girl or a job. Maybe down at Railhead they could find a use for that gun of yours ... but not here, and I can't see no girl.'

Swan smiled. 'You're probably right. I don't think I'm settled here like you.'

Cameron swallowed his scalding hot fish as easily as a kid drinking soda pop. 'Me, settled? Hell no, it's just a job. I'm too old for it but nothing happens around here. But one of these days I'll retire. I've a cabin in the mountains and a bit put by. I'll get me a yellow dog for company and take off there.'

'Make it a big dog,' Swan said.

'Why?'

'If you get snowed in and the food runs out, you can always eat the dog.'

Cameron cackled his appreciation of the old joke, then filled his mouth with hot fish again. Swan was suddenly weary of watching him eat: you could see the sinews under the skin as his mouth worked. He glanced over the clear water of the creek at the green bank on the other side and then at the big sky above. This wasn't bad country, hard but rich enough if you knew its ways.

But there was no point in hanging around longer. He wasn't sure why he had. No, tomorrow he'd set off for Railhead and the end of the spur line that would take him to the West Coast. Or back East. It was a strange name for a town, he thought, and a county seat at that. Probably they'd used the name so often when it was building that when it came to naming it formally they'd taken the easiest course and just kept on calling it Railhead. It was forty miles off. He needed to reckon on spending one night in the open and ...

'Deputy Cameron!'

Swan looked up. A kid was running towards them on this side of the creek. He looked tired and sweaty as if he'd run all the way from town, and very excited too.

Cameron put down the catfish he'd been about to bite into.

'Slow down.'

The boy stopped a few feet off them, took a breath.

'The mayor said to tell you there'd been a terrible accident.'

'What kind?'

'I'm not sure. They wouldn't let me see but Emma Smythe brought her rig into town driving like a madwoman and there's something wrapped up in the back. I was trying to see when Mayor Cummings gave me a dime to run for you.'

Cameron stood up. 'OK, lad, let's go get my horse. You can ride behind me if you want.'

71

'Yes, sir!'

Cameron looked across at Swan. 'Coming?'

Swan nodded, suspecting he wouldn't be riding for Railhead tomorrow after all. He didn't speculate about what had happened. Being a peace officer taught you not to. You always found out soon enough and you rarely liked it then. He stood up and, abandoning lines, pan and cooked catfish, he followed the old deputy and the boy.

Swan recognized Emma's rig tied up outside the undertakers. It was empty. Cameron led the way in.

It was a huge room with a table at the back, benches against two walls and seats everywhere. It was also used for council meetings, an unwholesome aspect of local democracy but practical. Emma was seated on the bench against the right wall, looking somehow very small and lost. Swan wanted to go over to her instantly and offer what comfort he could but something told him he didn't have the right.

Mayor Cummings approached the deputy. 'He's in the back room. Couldn't lay him out as he was. Daltoe says he can do something but I reckon it'll be a closed coffin job.'

'Let's have a look,' Cameron said.

They all three went from the big room to a much smaller room behind that smelled of iodoform and formaldehyde, altogether an unwholesome combination. Daltoe was in attendance, a large fat jolly man for an undertaker.

Wilse lay in a plain pine coffin on the trestle table. He looked very dead, his neck one huge bruise. Swan stepped forward, reached into the coffin and felt the back of his neck.

'It's intact,' Daltoe said. 'I checked too.'

So they hadn't even given him a drop, just left him to spin in the air, strangling. That could take a long time indeed.

'Who did it?' Cameron asked.

'The sister reckons it was Tarr. I see no reason to doubt her,' Daltoe said.

Neither did Swan. He was even sure Tarr had watched until the very end. It was usual to empty your guns into the lynched man as you left but even that final courtesy had been denied the boy.

'Bad,' Cameron said.

'Emma says they just left him for her to find, swinging,' Mayor Cummings, who looked like the undertaker he wasn't, said angrily. Swan

73

glanced at him; Cummings's cold green eyes and the set of his jaw suggested he was not a man to anger at will.

'So what about the burial?' Daltoe put in, looking at Cameron.

'That's for Mayor Cummings to say. He's the coroner round these parts. Ex officio.'

'Do we need to hold court?' Daltoe asked.

Cummings rubbed his angular chin. 'It's a killing. I reckon we do. Everybody's out there,' he indicated the other room, 'so I'll empanel a jury and get it over with. The verdict will be murder by Tarr and unknown associates.'

Cameron looked surprised. 'You think you'll get 'em to say that?'

'I'll direct 'em to, if need be,' Cummings said. 'It's true.'

Swan glanced once more at the boy he'd liked and who, he guessed, had liked him more, and walked back into the other room. He walked straight to Emma, took her by the shoulders and lifted her to her feet. 'Come on, we're getting out of here.'

'I'm not sure you should do that,' Cummings said from the door to the little room. 'She's a witness, after all.'

74

'She told you everything. Everybody here trusts you to relate that accurately and honestly, and by doing so you would be sparing the lady.'

The politician in Cummings couldn't resist either the compliment or the chance to appear gallant.

'If nobody objects ...'

Nobody did. Except maybe Emma herself, but it was only a flicker in her eyes and Swan led her from the huge dual-purpose room into the street. Where now? he asked himself, not regretting his high-handed action in the least. They were going to take an hour over it before bringing in the verdict the mayor had decided upon and during the course of that hour they'd labour the point of just how the boy had died. Emma probably realized but she didn't need it branding into her soul.

He led her to the hotel. She shied back; it wasn't usually a place for respectable women, but today was different. There was just one customer leaning on the bar, a drummer.

'I'd be obliged for some privacy,' Swan said. He said it very softly but the drummer looked at him once and left.

'Whiskey.'

75

The barkeep obliged.

'Drink that.'

'I—'

'Drink it,' Swan insisted and she did, coughing and spluttering at the raw strength of it. He led her to a table and sat her down, seating himself opposite. 'I'm sorry,' he said.

'He didn't come home last night,' Emma said. 'We looked for him on foot – it's not country for riding at night. And then this morning ...'

'It's not something you should ever have seen.'

'Why? That's what I can't understand. Why?'

In the last few days Swan had picked up enough local knowledge to understand very well. It was simple enough; the Bar X was trying to force everybody out. That was why Cummings would get his verdict: the 'shopkeepers' were all ranchers too, their properties run either by hired help or, more usually, their sons and daughters. If her parents had lived Emma would be one of them: the schoolteacher. No, she understood the reason well enough. She didn't understand how men could do such things. Swan did. He said nothing, just looked at her. He had only known her a few days but he somehow felt he could see into her soul. And it was agony to be able to do nothing for her.

'You brought it into the valley.'

'Brought what?'

'Death.'

'If you say so,' he said, keeping calm because he knew he had to for her sake.

'I'm sorry, it's not true. I just need to blame someone.'

'Blame those who did it,' he said reasonably.

'I'm tired,' she said suddenly and she looked as if she were about to collapse. He was out of his seat in a second, holding her. She was fainting with the weariness, the drink, and above all the horror of what she'd seen, had had to cut down Wilse and drive here with him in the rig. He picked her up and walked to the stairs.

'No women allowed—' began the barkeep but stopped very suddenly when Swan looked at him.

Swan put her in his own room for no very good reason. She was wearing an open-necked shirt and trousers so aside from loosening the belt he did nothing, even leaving her boots on. When she awoke she would be in no mood for fiddling with boots, and she wasn't wearing spurs.

He stood by the window and looked at her as she slept. She was pretty, though he had seen

77

prettier in dance halls, but so what? She was decent and kind and that was infinitely more important. And somebody had tried to break this butterfly on a wheel. That ought to make him very angry indeed, and he was surprised that it didn't. But he'd been angry for a long time indeed. Not even for her could he go back to that. He'd liked the boy but he wasn't his kin. In truth he was the kin of his late enemy. Let the law take its course.

What am I doing here? he asked himself suddenly. Not coming up with a useful answer he collected his saddle-bags and left her.

'She's asleep in my room,' he told the barkeep. 'Let her be but tell Mayor Cummings where she is when he's finished with his court business. OK?'

'Surely,' the barkeep said. 'A terrible business.'

As he walked out Swan reflected that the town was fully on the Smythes' side. What they'd do about it was another matter entirely.

It was ridiculous, sleeping with his horse in the stall, and yet it somehow seemed right. Tomorrow he'd go back to his old room. Or he'd move on. Maybe he had brought death into this high valley....

It made sense. These last few days hadn't. A range war was starting up – he'd seen them before too many times – and he didn't fool himself that right and truth would vanquish the ungodly. Usually it was the deeper pockets that prevailed.

He dug into his pocket and brought out the makings, rolling himself a cigarette out of the powdery tobacco.

'Don't smoke that in here,' Shaw said sharply.

Swan hadn't noticed him when he came in. The old man must have entered later, unheard. So the old Indian-fighter hadn't forgotten everything. But he was also carrying a pitchfork and suddenly Swan got the ridiculous idea he was being threatened – smoke and die!

'I wasn't intending to,' Swan said, biting off laughter. 'I was intending a bit of a walk before I turn in.'

Shaw rammed the pitchfork into a bale of hay. 'If you must be a damned fool, at least sleep on the bales, not in the stall. Horses are stupid, dirty animals.'

Swan said nothing. He'd noticed that his horse had been curry-combed to perfection and fed grain.

Then: 'You were at the inquest?'

Shaw shrugged. 'People die. Talking about it don't bring 'em back. Besides, I get to hear everything anyway.'

'And?'

'Murder by Tarr and unknown associates. Damned fools.'

'Why do you say that?'

'He's a killer, they aren't. Mice trying to bell the cat.'

'Maybe.'

'No maybe about it. They'll come to grief if they aren't very, very careful.'

'So will we all,' Swan said, and took his unlit cigarette outside.

The corral was empty. Swan leaned on the rail and looked at the town with the sunset fading behind it. Another year and what would there be here Probably all the same buildings – but people in them? It was hard to say.

'What's that you're smoking?'

Swan turned and saw Mayor Cummings standing beside him.

'I didn't hear you,' he said.

'Not wise for someone in your line of work,' Cummings said. 'But what are smoking?'

'Maybe the tobacco is a bit old.' He dropped the cigarette and crushed it under his heel.

'Have one of these,' Cummings said, tendering a cigar.

Swan took it. 'I'm usually chary of accepting cigars from civic dignitaries.'

'Rightly so. Never trust a politician. But take the cigar anyway, it don't commit you to nothing.' He lit a match and offered it to Swan, then lit up himself. 'It's a good view of the town. I often come here myself nights.'

The afterglow had almost gone and the pressure lamps were blazing, their tiny lights asserting the life of this little city on the high prairie.

'You got your verdict.'

'Never in doubt. But it's only words in an undertaker's parlour so far.'

'Cameron—'

'Cameron won't enforce it. I can't make him. He takes his orders from the sheriff in Railhead, when he bothers to give them.'

'And the sheriff?'

'You already know. A rustler got hung, so what else is new? If we arrest Tarr and send him for trial what would a Railhead jury of ranchers do to him?'

'Acquit,' Swan said. 'He wouldn't even need a good lawyer.'

'But it was murder.'

Swan said nothing. He was enjoying his cigar.

'The truth is,' Cummings went on, 'Cameron's virtually in retirement. I won't say he's cowardly ...'

'No,' Swan said, 'he's no coward. Tarr would kill him. He's not young any more but he's no coward.'

'You're young,' Cummings observed.

'It's a good cigar.'

Cummings laughed, then: 'You can go back to your room any time you want. The women have taken her in hand.. She's in the Lindstroms' house.' He paused. 'You did good to get her away from that ruckus.'

'I can see what you have in mind Mr Mayor. You can't control Cameron as he's the sheriff's deputy but as mayor you could appoint a town marshal ...'

'I'd prefer the term "chief of police".'

'Whatever, his remit would be to the town boundaries, no further.'

'He'd be a man with a legal gun.' Cummings paused. 'You're right. The cigar was a bribe. I want you for town marshal.'

I should say no, Swan thought. Before, the badge had always been a means to an end. To make what he did legal, and sometimes just to let him survive while he searched. But the search was over. He should leave.

'Which is the Lindstrom house?' he asked.

'That one there,' Cummings said, pointing. 'It's the one back of the saddler's.'

'Thanks.'

'And?'

'What are you offering?'

'I hadn't thought about it. Say a hundred a month.'

'Six hundred dollars.'

'A month? That's crazy!'

'For the job. It might take less than a month, maybe more.'

'It's a lot of money. The council will have to discuss it.'

'I'd want a free hand too. Advice, yes; interference, no.'

'You're asking a lot.'

'I'm being asked a lot.' Swan paused, then: 'Rivers has sold out, hasn't he?'

'How did you know?'

'He'd been here for years and no problems.

Suddenly Tarr is forcing everything and people die. It doesn't take a genius.'

'The word is he sold out to a group of financiers in Chicago and Tarr is now their agent. But that's a secret.'

'No,' Swan said. 'It has to be out in the open. If the Bar X take over the valley the town's finished. The buildings will still be there and maybe the saddler's and the saloon will still be occupied but that's all. People need to know that.'

'Yeah, you could be right.'

'What about the county sheriff? Whose side's he on?'

'His own – but nobody can buy him. Not even Chicago money. Perhaps he'd be more inclined to our side – we have votes in the election – but money buys lawyers. He'll stay strictly out of it. Strictly.'

'Fine.'

'All the same, there are thirty hands on the Bar X. Just one man ...'

'I wouldn't fight them on their terms,' Swan said. 'I know my business.'

'By all reports you do,' Cummings admitted.

Swan's cold smile was lost in the darkness. 'So?'

'The funeral's at ten tomorrow. The council can't decently meet until after. I'll tell you at noon.'

'OK.' Swan had no doubt what their decision would be. He almost wished they would reject his terms.

'What about Tarr. What—'

'I won't promise to kill anyone. But I will save your town for you. For six hundred dollars. And expenses.'

'What do you mean?'

'My hotel bill, any bar bills, and the odd little job. Nothing extravagant.' Swan laughed. 'Towns don't come that cheap. And thanks again for the cigar.' He noticed it was almost burnt out. He crushed it first with his fingers and then underfoot.

'I'll be back to tell you,' Cummings said, leaving.

Swan didn't watch him go. The stars were out, infinitely more numerous than their brighter imitators in the town, and infinitely colder. It had begun again. But now it was time to sleep. He'd be more comfortable in the hotel but somehow he couldn't bring himself to go. For this one night a palliasse of straw would serve just as well.

The Fifth Notch

*

The funeral had gone off well enough so far as Swan could tell. He'd been to very few: it had always seemed too much like gloating to attend those of the men he had killed. The preacher had read the words of the prayer book, the women had mostly cried, the men looked stern. Emma had looked small and lost. Somebody had found a black dress for her but she scarcely seemed to notice anything. She was alone in the world now, without kin, and the enormity of that was something Swan knew. She hadn't wept though, or even showed emotion. She had just stood there.

Swan got away first. There was nothing to say. He started back to the stable but changed his mind and went to the jail. Cameron was already there. He hadn't been at the funeral.

'Do you know about the marshal's job?'

'Yeah.'

'It's not final but I guess they'll take my terms.'

'Reckon so.'

'How do you feel about it?'

Cameron laughed. 'Have a look in back, boy. You'll find my bedroll and my shaving-kit too.

When I arrest anybody I dispossess myself. I'm too old for a range war and I know it.' He paused. 'But I knew the kid. Took him fishing a time or two. I'll move my bedroll and gear out and bunk with Shaw for a while.'

'There's no need—'

'Yes there is. A marshal needs an office – and a jail. The town owns it anyway, it's lent to the sheriff's office as a courtesy. I was thinking of taking off to that place in the mountains I mentioned but maybe not just yet.'

Swan remembered Mayor Cummings last night. Had he called Cameron a coward to his face? If so, he'd been very foolish indeed. But probably not. All the same, he'd come near.

'You were right,' Swan said. 'Courage isn't enough. You need speed too.'

Cameron looked at him long and hard, then: 'I take that very kindly, boy, very kindly.' He paused. 'I'll leave the keys on the desk. Use the guns as you like. They're sheriff's property but consider that his contribution. You'll get no other.'

'Will he interfere?'

'No. I sent him a telegram last night. No, he won't interfere.'

'I'm obliged.'

'For what?' Cameron said.

Swan didn't answer.

Mayor Cummings, now in his lawyer's office at the back of the general store, which he also part-owned, was not at his happiest. He was counting out double eagles. They quickly made two handsome piles on the desk.

'They didn't like it, Marshal,' he said, 'but there was no alternative.'

'If the worst comes to the worst, they'll get bought out. They'll take a loss but they'll live. I'll be dead.'

'An argument I put to them on your behalf, as it were,' Cummings said. 'They saw the weight of it but it didn't make the transaction happier for them.'

'You want to swear me in now?'

'I haven't worked out the proper form. In fact, the office hasn't been put into the city ordinance. Though I will write it in. Do you want to know what your powers are?'

'I reckon I'll be freer in exercising them if I'm not worrying about details.'

'So do I. Say: I do.'

'I do.'

'Sworn. If asked I'll testify it was done in due form. Do you likewise.'

'Yes, sir.'

'There's no badge ...'

'There's some spare deputy badges in the jail. One of them will do.' Swan took a pace forward and picked up both piles of double eagles.

'You wouldn't care to bank those, would you?' Cummings asked.

Swan laughed. 'A stray bullet might make the town six hundred dollars richer if I did. No, I don't think so.'

'What makes you think we wouldn't take them off your corpse?'

'I'm working for you,' Swan said simply.

Mayor Cummings just looked at him for a moment, then laughed. 'Maybe it was a good day indeed that you rode into Highville, boy.'

Swan didn't reply. This was the honeymoon period. Once the pain of paying you was over and done with they were pleased with themselves. They'd taken decisive action and it hadn't cost them anything but money.

There was a ruckus in the shop to the front. A moment later a tow-headed boy of about twelve

– Henry Lindstrom – burst in.

'She's leaving, Mayor Cummings. Pa said to run and tell you.'

Cummings stood up. 'Who's leaving, boy?'

'Emma Smythe. She changed out of the dress they gave her and started to harness up her rig. Says she's going home and nobody's going to stop her. Pa and Ma tried to talk her out of it but she won't listen so Pa says run and tell Mayor Cummings, he's never short of a word. Or a dozen. So I ran straight over but your clerk said you wasn't to be disturbed but Pa had said—'

'That's enough, lad,' Cummings said.' We'll be round to see to it.' He shook his head. 'Never short of a word ... reckon I'll take that as a compliment.' He looked to Swan who was watching the Lindstrom boy disappear back through the store. 'But maybe you can do the talking this time.'

Emma was checking that her shotgun was loaded when they got there. Swan watched her set it down again in the sheath at the side of the seatboard.

'Come down,' Mayor Cummings said. 'Please, Emma, come down..'

'I'm going home.'

'It's better for you to stay here.'

'I've stock to take care of and now there's just me and two old people to do it. I can't leave it to them.'

'I'll fetch them in for you,' Swan volunteered.

'Oh, you will, Marshal – and how much will you charge me?'

'The same as I did for getting you out from under your horse.'

She was silent for a moment, then: 'That cost me—'

'Don't say it,' Swan said quietly. 'For one thing, it's not true. For another, it's not worthy of you.'

She looked at him wide-eyed. 'You didn't find him swinging from a tree. He ...' She broke off. By this time Ma and Pa Lindstrom had come out again with the children. Swan wondered whether to clear them away. He knew how she felt: the impotent rage, the bitter anger, the need for revenge. He still knew it himself, even though the men he had hated were all dead and even the hatred had been cold by the time he killed them. Her agony had begun just yesterday.

'I want you to stay in town.'

'Is that an order, Marshal?'

'I'm just a peace officer, no more.'

'Then restore my peace. Kill Tarr for me,' She waited.

Swan said nothing.

'You won't, will you? You'll take their six hundred dollars but you won't kill him!'

Swan looked at the rest of them.

'Leave us.'

He was obeyed. Swan walked up and stood beside her. Even with her on the rig he didn't have to look up far. He said: 'I'm not a murderer, Emma. Maybe Tarr will end up dead but I won't promise you that. I can't.' He paused. 'I've killed men but I've kept to the rules—'

'The rules!'

'Shut up,' Swan said softly. 'You think you're the only person who's ever felt loss and hate? I'll tell you someday about ... but not now. I won't become a murderer for you. You don't know what you ask.'

Suddenly she was calm again. 'Maybe you're right. But I'm going anyway. What can I do in town? At least at home I can do something. I'll go mad if I stay here another minute.'

Swan knew she'd stay if he promised to kill Tarr for her. He'd sent everyone away partly for that reason. Marshal or not, if he threatened Tarr before witnesses and killed him, he could hang, but between just the two of them he could make the promise. And yet he found he couldn't utter the words. The rules were all that kept him sane: the difference between Tarr and himself.

He saw her looking at him, as if she'd read the mental battle from his face. She was waiting for the answer.

'No,' he said simply.

She touched the reins and the rig started to move. Swan stepped aside and watched as she drove away from Highville, whose suburbs were grass.

After a while he noticed Cummings standing beside him. 'She'll be all right, boy,' he said. 'They won't hurt a woman.'

'No,' Swan said, 'not even a jury of ranchers would believe it's right to lynch a woman for rustling.'

Five
THE EDGE

Crack! Swan fell down on one knee. *Crack!* He rolled. *Crack! Crack!* He stood up, put the gun back in its holster and walked the thirty yards to the bottles on the rise of ground. Three were shattered, one was on its side with the neck missing. That was the first shot after rolling. He'd gone high.

It was good enough. So far as he could judge the speed was fairly good too but bottles don't fire back at you. There was nothing like a touch of fear to speed you up.

From habit he took out his gun again and reloaded. He'd need to strip and clean it later but in the meantime he had to be ready. Nothing should happen today; little enough would happen tomorrow but at least it would start for real then.

It was an odd way of thinking about it – it was for real when *he* acted, not when Tarr killed a fifteen-year-old boy. But so it was.

He walked back to his horse, tethered to a rock forty yards off. You couldn't see the town from there, a great billow of prairie rose between them. That was why he'd chosen the place. He didn't want an audience. He had a rep but then so did many men and unless you saw them in action how did you know the great gunfighter wasn't a cowardly backshooter? Better if they believed he was. He needed an edge. And not just one: as many as possible. His shooting was one; the star was another; but the hate was gone, he needed something in its place. An idea crossed his mind. Yes, he'd do that.

He patted his horse's neck. 'Shooting doesn't worry you, girl, does it. You've been around me too long.' He noticed how good her coat was looking. Old Shaw at the livery didn't have a great deal of work to do but what he did, he did well. 'You'll be sorry when we leave here, girl,' he said as he mounted up. And just for a moment he thought of all the lonely old men he'd known who'd talked to their horses for want of other company.

'I can saw it,' Johnson the blacksmith said. 'Probably break a blade doing it but it can be done. But that close up it'll go off like a bomb-shell.'

'Like two bombshells,' Swan said. 'I don't want it for accuracy, just effect.'

Johnson smiled. He was a different type of blacksmith, small and wiry, his skin sallow from the forge.

'You want the stock down cut as well?'

'I wasn't going to ask.'

'Hell, I was a gunsmith of sorts once, during the war. I've done a bit since. I know what this is – a *pistola* as the Mexicans say. A horse pistol.'

'I'll leave it with you then. How much?'

'I thought you'd charge it to expenses.'

Swan smiled. 'That would be pushing it a bit.'

'Then take it as my contribution. I liked Wilse.' He paused. 'I got two kids. Tarr would hang them as easy.'

Swan nodded. So far the town was holding up well. But then very little had happened.

It started on Monday. That was the day the Bar X wagon rolled in for supplies. There were two on the wagon, not hired guns but plain cowhands. They were wearing guns but not intending to use them.

Swan watched from the other side of the street as they entered the store, then he walked slowly across.

'What the hell do you mean, can't let us have our order!' The man talking was the bigger of the two, a Swede by accent, tow-headed and strong as bear. His companion was utterly average.

'He means what he says. He's not stopping you, I am.'

'And who the hell do you think you are to do that, Deputy?'

'Not deputy. Marshal. And I've posted all Bar X men out of town.' He reached slowly into his shirt pocket and brought out a sheet of paper. 'Here, read it. Give it to your boss.'

'I'll read it,' the other man said, taking it quickly. The big Swede didn't object. If he were illiterate he didn't set much store by it. The smaller man read it out loud:

CITY OF HIGHVILLE
MARSHAL'S OFFICE:

On the grounds of public safety all persons working at the Bar X Ranch are hereby posted from town.

By authority

Jack Swan, City Marshal.

The big Swede laughed. 'You're going to stop us?'

'If I have to.'

The big man took a pace forward. He made no move towards his gun. It was as if he'd forgotten it was there. Swan didn't want to draw on him but he had no intention of getting into a fist-fight with him either.

'Did Tarr tell you to attack the marshal?' he asked.

The power of the name stopped the Swede.

'Let's leave it, Karl,' the smaller man said. 'Let Tarr sort it out. I've heard the marshal's name before. He's got a rep.'

'I ain't no gunfighter,' Karl said, thinking about it.

'It's not personal,' Swan said. 'It applies to the whole Bar X.'

But Karl decided differently. Swan had thought he might, though he had expected a physical attack. He had devised a very ungentlemanly response too. Instead Karl went for his gun.

He was muscly and slow. Swan could have put a bullet in him before the gun was fully out of its holster. But it would have had to be a crippling or a killing shot. Karl wouldn't back down.

Swan put his gun almost in the smaller man's face.

'Holster up or I'll kill your *compadre*.' He hoped that was the relationship.

Karl was nonplussed. The evident threat to his friend flummoxed him. It was totally unexpected.

'For God's sake, Karl!' the other man said, suddenly white-faced.

Karl hesitated a moment longer and then the gun disappeared into its holster. Swan's did likewise. He stepped back in an unspoken invitation for them to leave. Once they were on the sidewalk, Swan added:

'Come into town again armed and I'll kill you, unarmed, and I'll jail you.'

Neither looked back.

'So it's started,' Mayor Cummings said from the back of the store, standing in the door of his office. 'Would you really have killed the little guy?

Swan nodded. 'I didn't know how fast he was. He could have shot me. Karl was so slow I could afford to take him last.'

Cummings cleared his throat sceptically. 'I thought your canon was set against murder.'

'Not murder. The law of common purpose. One drew on me, the other would have.'

'That's thin ... but arguable.'

'They wouldn't have argued,' Swan said and turned on his heel, well satisfied. Cummings had helped unknowingly. The story would get around and Tarr almost certainly had a spy in town. For now it was even useful to have a conduit to the enemy. Not that he would have needed to kill either. He'd had time. Karl had obviously never pulled the trigger on a man in his life and the other fellow hadn't made a move. Of course, if he had he would have killed him along with Karl. That was within the rules. As it was, he'd gained a reputation for utter ruthlessness by doing nothing but drew his gun. It was for Tarr now to up the ante.

Swan took the completed *pistola* from the black-smith. The barrels were very short indeed and the leatherwork was very simple: a strip belt and an open holster attached directly to it. Swan hadn't expected the holster: a *pistola* was a weapon you normally carried in your hand for instant use. When he wore a badge Swan didn't go in for any such nonsense as fast draws on Main Street. He was fast but a lawbreaker might be faster. The whole point of a fast draw was to give the game some semblance of fairness and cheat the hangman. Sheriff's and marshals never got hung. Sometimes they got shot, never hung.

'Hell of a gun,' Johnson said. 'Wouldn't care to draw against it myself.'

'That's the whole point,' Swan said.

Then came the waiting. The trick was to still be the hunter even as others thought of you as prey. He managed it because he knew just how good he was at this job and just how bad most of the 'gunnies' who killed for pay were. The lightning draw and shoot-out at noon did happen but more often than not it was backshooting with shotguns.

He leaned back on the chair and surveyed his kingdom. It was about the smallest he had ever worked in. And the least active. Cameron was a tax-collector more than anything and as Swan wasn't the deputy but the city marshal, that left him nothing to do but show himself now and then.

'Use some company?'

Swan looked up, saw Cameron in the doorway. 'I was just thinking of you.'

'Something good?'

'I was envying you your tax-collecting. Something to do.'

'It's not the time,' Cameron said.

'I know.' He stood up. 'Let's get out of here. Fishing?'

'Why not? I'll get the tackle.'

Swan paused to buckle on the *pistola* and slip a few extra shotgun cartridges into his pockets.

The fish weren't biting but neither man cared. Cameron was telling him how he'd got into the business. His father had been a deputy in Illinois. He'd come West and kept up the tradition. 'It beats punching cows.'

'Not if they're your own.'

'If you can afford a ranch.'

'I can,' Swan said.

'So why don't you?'

And so he had ended up telling Cameron how he'd begun. Of the burning.

'I'd heard something of the sort,' Cameron admitted. 'But why?'

'Missouri just after the war. Ostensibly it was about land – my father was a lawyer – but it was paying off old scores too. I didn't go into the rights and wrongs of how it started. The wrong of the way it ended was enough for me.' He paused. 'There were five of them, the ringleaders. It was no secret, but there was nothing I could do about it then. Or much of anything. I was all burned up. When I could walk again it turned out my father's estate had just about paid the medical bills. I couldn't argue. I was just a kid. They found me a job on a farm.

'The farmer wasn't given to human charity or human feeling of any kind. I slept in the barn and worked like a horse. And pretty much ate like one. I hated him.'

'And?'

'Did I kill him? No. I just upped and left. All I took with me were the clothes on my back and a dodger with names on it. I reckon the town was on the side of the burners, not my pa, but for form's sake they'd posted a lousy twenty-dollar reward for the five men to be brought to trial. Not that they ever expected to pay out but I saw even then that it made killing them legal.'

'More or less.'

Swan understood his reservations. A dodger – a wanted poster – wasn't a warrant; it wasn't even a legal document of any kind, just a poster issued by a law-officer. But nobody questioned them so it didn't matter.

'I didn't rush at it. I'd learned patience lying on a bed while a drunken doctor fed me laudanum, and waited for me to die.' He paused. 'I'd no intention of dying.'

'No, I reckon not,' Cameron said.'

'After I left the farmer I moved westward, riding the rails sometimes. Finally I stopped in a cowtown, got a job sweeping at the saloon. I learned to shoot. And then I got a job sweeping out the jail.' He lapsed into silence.

Cameron broke it. 'They're all dead?'

'Yeah. One to fever, the other four I shot. I did it fair. I didn't backshoot any of them.'

'Hell, after what they did, who cares?'

Swan suddenly realized he didn't. That he would have backshot them if that had been the

107

only way. Maybe that would have made him a dime-novel villain but so what? Yet the knowledge didn't make him feel happier about himself.

'So why are you here? The girl?'

Swan said nothing. He could tell him ... but something held him back. He shrugged.

'Maybe you should have kept riding,' Cameron said. 'Hell, I know your rep but so do the Bar X bunch. Do you think they'll come at you fair?' He paused. 'I know this. There's no certainty in a gunfight.' He broke off, then: 'Mayor Cummings reckons I'm a coward.'

'I don't.'

'Maybe you're wrong and he's right. I haven't got the stomach for it no more. When you start going grey and your digestion's not what it was, you feel different about things.'

'Knowing your limitations isn't cowardice. It's good sense. I just walked into it. But I can't walk away. And I don't intend getting killed, not one bit of it.'

Cameron looked at him, smiling wryly: 'I reckon it's the Bar X that's got to worry.'

When the Bar X did finally turn up in town it was from the direction of Railhead and in the form of a small, dapper man called Lecamus, Attorney Lecamus. Apparently Tarr had been burning up the telegraph with messages to his Chicago bosses. Lecamus was the result.

Swan first met him when Mayor Cummings called him to his office at the back of the general store. Lecamus was there, fat, snub-nosed and smiling.

'We've a problem,' Cummings said.

'I'll explain if you wish it, Mr Mayor,' Lecamus sad. 'I've brought and served a writ from the circuit judge injuncting you from posting out the Bar X personnel. You had no legal basis whatso-ever to do it.'

The mayor just shrugged.

Swan smiled. 'Consider it done, Mr Attorney. I'm a peace officer. I obey the law.'

'I'm delighted to learn it. I can tell my clients they can come into town any time they want?'

'Naturally,' Swan said, aware that the mayor was looking at him oddly. 'There's just one proviso.'

'Which is?'

'Do you want to tell him, Mayor?'

'Me – I ...'

'I'll do it then,' Swan said. 'The mayor would

have told you the city council are meeting this evening to pass a new city ordinance. No guns to be carried within the city limits. Correct, Mr Mayor?'

'Yes indeed.' Cummings was smiling now.

'I'm not sure that that isn't breaking the spirit of the writ,' Lecamus said.

'I don't see the connection,' Swan said. 'It applies to everybody.' He paused. 'Peace officers excluded, of course.'

'And I don't recall the circuit judge said we couldn't promulgate our own city ordinances, did he?' Mayor Cummings put in.

'Of course not!'

'Then the Bar X boys are free to come in any time. Unarmed.' Cummings' smile broadened. 'Today, of course, they could come in armed but I don't reckon you'll have time to tell them before we pass the ordinance.'

'Very irregular,' Lecamus said.

'No,' Swan said, 'quite legal. You can tell them from me they'll be quite safe, provided they obey the ordinance. Presuming, of course, the council passes it.'

'You can count on that!' Cummings said.

Lecamus stood up.

110

'Going back to Railhead?' Cummings asked, now rather too obviously enjoying himself.

'No,' Lecamus said, mustering up his dignity. 'I thought I'd see my clients. You don't object to that, do you?' He was looking at Swan as he said it.

'I just keep the peace,' Swan said. 'You can tell the boys that. Though maybe you'd be safer not going.'

'A threat?'

'Not at all, just advice. I was meaning that at the Bar X I hold no sway. I am city marshal, no more. And your clients are—'

'I have nothing to fear from my clients!'

'I trust so,' Swan said and walked out. Lecamus was a fool and whoever had sent him was a fool. You don't stop a war with legalisms. He found himself outside the stables looking towards the Smythe ranch and the way he had come into the valley and the town. The war proper had been delayed but it was still on. It would come to blood.

Six
THE GUNMAN

Lecamus felt very uncomfortable. It was not down to the jolting buggy-ride over a rutted trail and through those twin pillars of eroding sandstone called the Iron Gates that gave the only practical access to the Bar X ranch, though it had set his joints aching, but to the man facing him.

He'd met Tarr in Chicago when he'd come with Rivers to see Sean Flynn at the Metropole hotel when Flynn had bought out the Bar X. It had seemed a good deal then: buy out the valley and increase the cattle deliveries eightfold. A good deal: he'd said as much to Flynn, never thinking he'd be sent out here. Even if he had known, the thought of meeting Tarr wouldn't have worried him. Standing awkwardly in the plush hotel suite in a set of ill-fitting store-bought clothes he'd been nobody to fear. But he was now.

He'd the same look in his eyes Flynn used to

have when he'd been a saloon-keeper and gang-
ster, before he'd become a legitimate business-
man. Not that it had left him entirely even now,
but Tarr had it in spades. A very appropriate
suit, Lecamus thought.

'Your advice!' Tarr said. 'Do you think I need
your advice?'

'Maybe you do,' Lecamus said. 'After all, we
both work for Mr Flynn.'

'He promised me five thousand dollars—'

'When the deal was complete.'

'Right. Until then, it's down to me. And if you
think I'm going to let myself be shot by that
quickfire marshal to please you, be damned to
you!'

'The writ ...'

'Much good to me with lead in my belly.'

Lecamus fidgeted in the hard wooden chair.
The Bar X was an imposing house from the
outside, white-painted with a wooden portico, a
touch of fake antebellum architecture planted
out here in the West, but the furnishings didn't
match; just hard chairs and unpolished tables.
And what the beds would be like....

'Well?' Tarr was staring down at him. 'What
does Flynn want me to do?'

'Mr Flynn's only interested in the cattle deliveries. That was made plain in Chicago. You have a free hand otherwise, within the law.'

Tarr laughed. 'Flynn doesn't mind if I hang so long as he gets his cattle. Neither do you.'

Lecamus was slow in denying it and Tarr reached down and grabbed him by the cravat, twisting hard.

'For God's sake ...'

Tarr released him, smiled. 'I could hang you. I hanged a boy not long since. You should've seen him kick. And there were people to care about him. Who cares about you Mr Attorney?'

'Mr Flynn—'

'Is only interested in money.'

Lecamus began to shake.

Tarr laughed. 'Hell, I was just joking. I've nothing against you, save for the way you look.' He laughed again. 'Have a drink.' He indicated the bottle on the table. 'I've got cows to see to. Talk to you later.' Then he left.

Lecamus looked at the bottle but made no motion towards it. He needed a clear head for the drive back. He wasn't spending the night in this madhouse. Damn Tarr for the madman he was – and damn Flynn for thinking to make money out of him. He took a deep breath and realized his curse was unnecessary. If ever a man was on his way to hell, it was Tarr.

And the sooner he was away, the better. He rubbed his neck. The hanging business hadn't been exactly idle talk. Tarr's eyes had lighted up at the very thought.

Lecamus got to his feet and, for all he had taken no drink, started quickly but unsteadily out of the room and off the Bar X.

Tarr made his move two days after Lecamus's hasty departure. He sent a hired killer into town. There were two cowhands with him but as soon as the party arrived they entered McGaye's bar and made a point of handing their guns over to the barman, a trifle less formal than handing them in at the marshal's office but still a usually acceptable practice.

A boy brought the news, Anthony McGaye, about fourteen and excited. Swan noticed how the boy looked at him. He'd seen it before. Am I looking at a dead man?

'I'll be there,' he told young McGaye who promptly scuttled off leaving Swan wondering if this time the boy had the right of it. He picked up

the holstered *pistola*, took it out of the holster.
Its place was in his hand. He went out holding it,
knowing more or less what was coming.

The three of them were waiting for him
outside the bar, their guns back in place. It was
an old trick, have a drink and then leave with
your guns. The barman wasn't about to argue.
And then the law arrived expecting no trouble
and without reinforcements.

He looked them over and kept up his pace.
None of them had drawn. It was meant to be
'fair' except the odds would be three to one.

But old tricks had old answers to them and
only very stupid people played them. The hired
gun was in the centre, his dark suit and the
custom rig of his gunbelt giving away his profes-
sion. He was flanked by the two cowhands, who'd
probably never shot at anything but a rattler
before, and missed. Maybe they'd shoot when it
came to it but never first.

Swan stopped ten feet from them, raising and
cocking the *pistola* as he did so.

'I'm giving you five seconds to drop your
gunbelts.' He kept the pistola aimed at belly-
level, centred on the gunman. 'It's loaded with
buckshot and at this range the spread would cut

you in half. If Tarr's paying you enough to risk that, draw.'

And suddenly it was over. The would-be killer was only too anxious to unbuckle his belt, dropping it in the dust. The buckaroos took their time: the *pistola* wasn't aimed directly at them. But they didn't dally overmuch.

'Now leave,' Swan said.

The gunhand made to pick up his gunbelt.

'Leave it.'

He was a tall, thin man with dark, dead eyes and snaggly teeth, and a look of pure dark hatred on his face. But leave it he did. He turned and walked away. The other two followed suit. Swan watched them go, patiently waiting. He took the opportunity to switch the *pistola* to his left hand and draw his Colt with his right. When he was about thirty feet away the tall gunman turned, raised his arm.

Swan shot, catching him in the middle of the chest. He fell like a sack of potatoes, something small and silver falling into the dust of the street beside him: a .44 Derringer.

The two cowhands turned too, but took the precaution of raising their hands. Swan knew some lawmen would have shot them all just to be on the safe side.

'If you're carrying a holdout gun, drop it,' Swan said.

'I'm not,' one of them said, stuttering.

'Me neither.'

Swan believed them.

'Then go.'

The stutterer started back for their horses on the hitching rail.

'Leave the horses,' Swan said.

'But—'

'They could be stolen from the Bar X. Mr Tarr can call in and collect them. You walk.'

The humiliation was complete. They started walking, gunless, horseless, humiliated – and towards Railhead. They obviously had no more stomach for facing Tarr than facing him. God help their feet when they get there, Swan thought. But he knew they'd never trouble him again. He had the Indian sign on them.

Except the truth was he'd simply been readier to kill than they had, gunman included.

Suddenly Swan turned and walked back to his office. People were already looking at him through their windows. Soon they'd be coming out to congratulate him and he didn't want that.

I ought to feel elated, he thought. Or ashamed. But what he felt at killing a man and humiliating two others was even worse.

He felt nothing at all.

The bottle on the desk was three quarters empty but Swan wasn't drunk. He wanted to be but he was just fuzzy, and that only around the edges. He swore bitterly: drink was supposed to be an escape, town drunks all hiding a terrible secret from themselves, to be lost daily courtesy of two pints of bourbon. Except it wasn't true. You also needed to be weak so it wasn't a choice open to him.

'He'd've killed you,' Cameron said from the doorway.

Swan looked up. 'Eh?'

Cameron glanced meaningfully at the bottle.

Swan laughed 'I wasn't thinking of him. He took his pay to kill me and for once he didn't earn it. Or maybe he did. In full.' He paused. 'Damn him.'

'So why the booze?'

Swan looked up. 'You really want to know?'

'Why not?'

Swan told him.

122

Cameron walked over and took the bottle. 'Do you mind?'

'Finish it. It doesn't work for me.'

'You expect too much. Hell, you think too much.'

'Do I?'

'Sure. Who are you, God Almighty punishing unto the fourth generation? Or even the second? What did Emma Smythe ever do to hurt you? Her father's dead. If he'd been alive you'd've killed him, whatever.'

'Would I?'

'Oh, yes, and you know it. The law, the rules – it's so much talk. You've been killing for vengeance. Maybe you're right, maybe not. But it's over. You can't kill the dead, just the living.' He wiped the neck, took a swig. 'I remember him well. He wasn't much of a killer. A small man with a haunted look to him. He'd come out West to start over and he succeeded. He had a decent wife and two good kids and fever took him, not your bullets.'

Swan said nothing.

'Do you love her?'

'How do I know?'

'Why else are you here? You could have ridden

123

on. California. Or Oregon. But you didn't. You love her all right, and no reason not to. She's a fine girl.'

'She asked for my help and I sent her away.'

'To kill Tarr. No, you didn't refuse. You just went your own way about it. I know about posting men out of town. They always come in. Just like Bluebeard's wife – the locked door's the only one that's worth opening.'

'So why hasn't he?'

'Because he's afraid of you and he's playing it safe. There's money in it for him.' Cameron took another, larger swig. 'You've probably been wondering who was his spy in town.'

'Yes.'

'Now you know.'

It made sense. Why should any one of the townsfolk put himself out of business? And a deputy would come cheaper. He looked at Cameron. 'The sheriff's in it too.'

'Of course. This is a small town to have a deputy to itself, and he needs money too. As for me, I ain't got no pension. It's no excuse—'

'Forget it,' Swan said. 'Half the lawmen in this country are on the take in one way or another.'

'Thanks,' Cameron said. Then: 'There wasn't supposed to be any killing. Some financier in

Chicago's behind it – Flynn. You heard of him?'

Swan nodded but said nothing. Flynn was a pimp who'd made good – or rather, rich. A very nasty piece of work. But he was in Chicago and that was a long way away.

'That's it,' Cameron said. 'If you want to call me out …'

'Don't be a fool. I undertook to save the town for money, that's all. And I will. Maybe that's not much better. But has Tarr heard about what happened to his men?'

'Yes.'

'Then you've done me a favour. He's no choice now but to come in himself.'

'Maybe.' Cameron paused, then fingered his own deputy's badge. He said:

'Raise your right hand.'

'What?'

'Your hand!'

Swan raised his hand.

'Do you undertake to uphold the laws of this state and county.'

'Why not?'

'You're now a special deputy. What use it'll be against Tarr, I don't know, but if you kill him you surely won't hang.'

125

'How will the sheriff take this?'

'Not badly. He took his money up front.'

As did you, Swan thought, but he couldn't bring himself to condemn the old man. There were too many little ranches in this valley. Time would surely curtail their number, whatever.

Cameron bent to open the left-hand drawer of the desk, took out a form. 'I'll confirm it in writing. I'll turn in my badge too, though I'll have to go Railhead to do it.'

'Keep it if you want. I'll not say anything.'

Cameron looked up a moment. 'Thanks – but I'll do it anyway. I was a pretty fair lawman once. Maybe if I resign now I can remember those years, not these.'

Swan was no longer paying him any attention. Tarr would be coming in. That was important. And it felt better now he had told someone about Emma. He wondered if he should tell her everything. Probably not. Besides, it would be hard for her knowing her father was a murderer. Yes, that about clinched it.

'There …' Cameron began, handing him the completed form. He was interrupted by the McGaye boy shouting from the sidewalk outside:

'Come out and see, Marshal, come out and see!'

126

It took them a few moments to get outside to see the reason for all the noise but finally they did. It was getting dark and the smoke was almost lost in the gloom but you could see the flames, tiny flickers of light on the horizon. So Tarr did have one more option besides coming in.

'Emma,' Swan said softly, almost under his breath.

Seven
THE NIGHTRIDE

Shaw at the livery complained bitterly but Swan was in no mood to brook delay and with Cameron, now armed with a Winchester, to back him, a rig was soon provided, a well-endowed one with two horses to pull and another pair tied to the back as spares if either of the other two found gopher holes in the night or simply tired.

'Who' paying?' Shaw demanded.

'The town's paying,' Cameron said. 'See Cummings.'

Swan didn't add anything. It was odd how Cameron's act of betrayal was so quickly forgotten – and yet, why not? He hadn't betrayed him, just the town. And why should either of them care about a town that would discard either of them without a second's hesitation when their use ran out? Cameron was with him now and that was all that counted.

The journey was harrowing. Swan's instincts

were to go hell for leather over the rough trail but he also fully intended to get there so he had to hold back. The moon was near full and that was a help but the pace was still agonizingly slow.

The horses were nervous. Swan could have whipped them into going faster but he knew that even two spare horses weren't enough for that game: he could well have used up ten. In the distance there was nothing to be seen now; the flames had burnt themselves out and the smoke was lost in the dark.

Cameron spelled him at driving from time to time and then he sat on the jolting seat of the buckboard and smoked cigars, trying for calm. He was pretty sure he caught the appearance of it; he also knew Cameron wasn't fooled. Finally he said:

'Do you think—'

'I don't think,' Cameron said. 'I wait and see. You've no doubts now, have you?'

'Damn you, you know how I feel!'

Cameron grunted. 'Tell her sometime.'

'Then you think she's alive?'

'I don't reckon anybody's dead till I see 'em laid out,' Cameron said, 'and even then I've been known to be sceptical.'

Swan laughed despite himself. Gallows humour was better than no humour at all. What made everything worse was that he'd never really cared about anyone since the burning, except for the five names. Ironic that it was for someone who shared one of those names that he cared now. Images of what Tarr might have done flicked across his mind, tightening his stomach. But it wasn't Tarr he thought about, only her.

'I'll drive,' he said.

They were six miles off by dawn Cameron insisted they stop and change horses, letting the first pair go loose to make their own way back to the livery. They had given good service. Then, with a relatively fresh but rather spooked pair before them, they drove like madmen to the ranch.

Cameron checked his Winchester. Maybe he'd made the wrong choice himself. In his haste he'd just brought the new-minted *pistola* to supplement his normal sidearm. But it would serve.

They could see the ranch now and suddenly Swan felt sick at heart. The house was burnt down to the ground though the barn still stood. He could see no movement whatsoever.

'We'll know one way or another soon enough,' Cameron said.

Swan was grateful he'd omitted the prefatory *Steady!* Now it was taking all his strength to keep even the semblance of calm. His heart seemed to be trying to punch through his ribs and his stomach was like a washboard. He'd never felt fear like this before, not since the first burning. . . .

At last they drew level with the remains of the house. He tugged gently on the reins and leapt down, looking about desperately. The house was now just a burnt pattern on the ground but there were no obvious bodies.

'I'll check the barn,' he said.

Don't run! he told himself. He managed a few unhurried paces, then started running, the *pistola* slapping against his thigh, supremely useless. He wanted to call out her name but somehow he couldn't. Then he found himself before the barn door.

It was wet. The fire? Sometimes ... He reached out and touched it. No, somebody had thrown buckets of water over it. To save it. Maybe the Bar X buckaroos? A spare barn on the property was always useful. But he doubted that.

He pushed it slowly open.

She was there, sat with the two old people on the straw. Her clothes were filthy and her face was grey from the smoke except where tears had forced little runnels through it.

'Emma,' he said.

And suddenly she was up and in his arms and crying, all seemingly in one motion, and he held her, near to tears himself.

Except he'd long since got out of the habit of weeping. For all he had wept with the pain of his burns. Yet better that than this night again. But now it was daylight and Emma was in his arms, safe and well.

'Thank God,' he said softly.

'There were six of them, including Tarr. I tried to hold them off – Esposito helped – but they threw coal-oil on the house and set it alight. We got out the back and ran to the barn.'

'Why didn't you ride off?'

'I might have outridden them but neither Esposito nor Mamacita could.'

Swan noted that she said it matter of factly, not proudly, as if she saw no reason to boast that she wouldn't ever abandon her friends.

He said: 'And he made no move to set the barn alight?'

'The water …' She shook her head. 'No, that was us. Sparks from the house. We did that when he'd gone. No, he just shouted to us to leave or he would kill us. Then he rode off.'

'Six of them,' Swan said. He looked to Cameron.

'Probably all he has left. The real buckaroos will have been deserting in droves. They're cowhands, not killers.'

'I thought he was going to kill us,' Emma said, grasping Swan's hand.

'No,' Swan said. But Tarr had risked her life nonetheless. He had set her home ablaze with her in it. That he would never forgive. But he probably never intended to kill her. Killing a boy and calling him a rustler was something he could get away with. Kill a woman and he could well hang. He still wanted to take over the valley and keep it. And with Flynn's backing, maybe he could. Gunmen were cheap in Chicago. All Tarr had to do was get rid of one man, the new town marshal….

And suddenly he saw it all. He was being tempted. Tarr had jumped to the right conclusion for the wrong reasons. And maybe he was still jealous too.

'He's challenging me,' Swan said. 'He expects me to go and arrest him. Except I'd be out of my jurisdiction, acting *ultra vires* as the lawyers say.'

'Not any more,' Cameron said and then thought better of it. 'Don't be a fool, man!'

'What are you talking about?' Emma asked.

Swan looked at her, tired and dirty, happy and sad at the same time. And now confused. The devil who her father was! But Tarr had set fire to her home with her in it and that was something he could never forget. His gun had been crying out for that fifth notch. Tarr would do very nicely.

'I'm going after him,' he said.

'No!' Emma looked suddenly terrified.

'She's right,' Cameron said.

'If we wait, we lose. You said yourself, the sheriff has been paid to look the other way. That hasn't changed. What do I do? Take a town posse out to the Bar X? Shopkeepers against gunmen? Tarr's cruel and he's a bit crazy but he's clever too. He'll not come into town now.' He looked hard at Cameron. 'Will he?'

'No.'

'So what do you suggest?'

'Take her with you and go.'

'I don't run,' Swan said. 'I never have. I'll not start now.'

'What are you talking about?' Emma asked, almost shouting. But she knew.

'Tarr wants me dead or gone. Either way he wins. But it works just as surely the other way. With him dead, it's over. Flynn needs Tarr. With him gone he'll just cut his losses. Tarr made it local. The sheriff would never allow a Chicago killer to come and take over. It'd be just too raw.'

Cameron nodded.

'So it's between Tarr and me, always was.'

'He'll kill you,' Emma said, horror in her voice.

'No,' Swan contradicted her – with conviction. He was no longer in the least uncertain. The job he had taken on so long ago against the arsonists had just been made unfinished again. It was inconceivable it wouldn't be finally completed.

She saw the certainty in his face but it didn't make her less afraid. He smiled at her and walked to the nearest stall.

'I'll take a horse from here. Cameron, you take all three of them back to town. Nobody'll bother you.'

Cameron nodded.

'No!'

Swan lifted a saddle from the rail. 'I'll be back. Whether you want to see me then is up to you.'

She looked suddenly bemused.

As he led the saddled horse to the door he turned to her. 'Don't worry. I've done this before.' He looked to Cameron. 'On the ride back, tell her about me. Tell her why I came here.' He paused, then: 'I'd be obliged.'

'I don't understand any of this,' Emma said. 'But I know he'll kill you like he killed Wilse. He's ...' she sought for a word but could manage no more than 'a killer.'

'So am I,' Swan said and left abruptly.

Eight
THE TRAP

He was riding into a trap. There was only one practicable route from the Smythe ranch to the Bar X: through the Iron Gates. He'd seen them at a distance when he first came to the valley, an enormous stone doorway.

How many men would Tarr have left there – three or four? After the business in town he would really have had to stack the odds just to get them to do it. But he wouldn't have stayed himself. He'd be back now at the ranch just in case they failed. With one man as back-up – and backshooter.

How easy it was to think like such a man as Tarr. Or maybe they really were alike, stone killers both of them. Swan rejected the idea. He always had. He was no murderer. He even had the law on his side: he was a marshal and deputy both. But most of all he had right on his side against the house-burner.

143

The trap was no worry. They never were when you knew. Quite the opposite. He took the route he had used with Emma when she had been hurt, then rode back on to the main trail. Thereafter he didn't know the land but he'd seen the maps in Cameron's office and he'd always been good with maps.

The route he'd chosen was an unlikely detour but for an extra ten-mile ride it brought him round the other side of the Bar X. Now the four men he'd bypassed were no longer of any concern to him. With their paymaster dead they would simply leave and be glad of the chance. Men such as Tarr inspire no loyalty.

He found himself thinking about Emma. How would she feel when she knew that he had come here to kill her father? He'd decided before on saying nothing but better to lose her than start with lies.

That thought made him afraid, for he knew he might. She wanted Tarr dead all right for what he had done to Wilse but she would know he wasn't avenging him. He'd liked the boy but he had the wrong name for that. And so had she.

She'd also know that if her father had been alive he would have killed him. She had pride too. And a hatred of guns very suitable in a would-be school teacher....

Of course Tarr could solve the problem by killing him. It was easy to despise him because he enjoyed cruelty and was more than a little crazy, but he was cunning in his craziness.

He reached the trail and looked back the way he'd come, to the place where he'd first seen her. He rather fancied stopping and remembering, maybe having a smoke, but he didn't have the makings and his cigars were all gone, gone in the night.

He rode north, only the map in his mind and the smell of burning wood and creosote in his nostrils.

It was late in the afternoon when Swan finally saw the Bar X ranch house. It was set in a depression between low hills with a few stunted, wind-broken trees set atop them. It was obvious Indians had posed no problem when it was built. As a fort it would be woefully lacking but as it was the wells would have been easily dug and there was shelter from the wind. He stood by his horse on the most northerly of the hills, lost in the foliage to anybody looking up, and planned his way down.

There was nobody about that he could see but that only meant nobody was moving about. He went through the calculation again in his mind. Tarr and one other. No more.

The easiest way in was on the trail from the Iron Gates coming in from the east which would have the advantage of setting his shadow unseen behind him, but it was also the usual way. He couldn't risk it. From here? There were acres of green, open land. He was certain to be spotted. Likewise from the south.

So from the west it was. There was an outcropping there which had collapsed into a talus slope lower down, a great shambles of broken rock. He couldn't risk that but beside it were many large, outrider rocks for cover and by the time he got there it would be in shadow. Thereafter it was only a hundred yards to the nearest barn....

He drew his Colt, checked it over. Then the *pistola*. Finally he checked that his horse was well tethered. It was time to start moving but he was strangely reluctant to do so. This made number five, the last one. The one he'd lost and found again. Even if Tarr hadn't been in Missouri he still fitted the bill better than ever Smith would have. He was a burner of houses, a killer ... but worst of all, he had put Emma in danger.

Suddenly the old reluctance was gone and he started moving, keeping to the reverse slope of the hills.

The descent was easier than it had looked; he kept close to the rock fall, picking his way between the massive boulders whose shadows loomed black before them, growing too as the sun dwindled away in the west. He was sure he could not be seen.

He waited as the shadow deepened and then flowed towards the barn and its even deeper shadows. The mock antebellum house was just a dark mass now, no window lighted, yet he was certain Tarr was waiting for him within.

That thought made him go a little colder than the coming night itself; the scars on his back began to ache; a smell of burning, very faint, was in his nostrils; and his movements became lighter, more controlled. He moved swiftly across the now shadowed ground to the barn and then on to the house. A door stood ajar, almost an invitation.

He avoided it, looking instead to the windows. Two were open. He chose the nearer, peered into

147

the dark interior, seeing nothing. He opened the window to the full and stepped inside, even more cautious now that he was in a dark room with furniture to knock over. But there wasn't any: it was just an empty room.

Maybe Tarr had left all his men at the Iron Gates. He moved into the corridor, almost believing it, when he saw the flash of the knife.

The dark was almost total, only a few glimmers of light penetrating from the window in the room behind him but the blade caught them. The man behind it was just a dark mass.

It would have been easy simply to shoot him but this wasn't Tarr, he was sure, and he didn't want to alert him. He watched the blade rise and then come down at him. He reached to catch the descending wrist.

It was bad technique, striking down: the bony structure of the body didn't yield easily to a downward attack. But a knife is always dangerous.

Now, the thousands of hours he had practised with a gun, drawing and shooting, drawing and shooting, paid off. He felt the bony wrist between his fingers, held on to it for life itself, not trying to stop the downward strike but completing it, forcing it away from himself and towards the barely distinguishable body of the man before him.

For a second the knife was fixed in the space between them; the assailant need merely drop it, pull away. But he didn't. He held on.

Swan reached forward with his other hand, catching the arm at biceps level, levering in backwards now, and the knife stayed clamped in the other's hand until it slapped against his belly.

He made no sound but the knife left his hand, stayed there, stuck obscenely in the assailant. Swan relaxed his grip, his hand darting for the hilt. He caught it, jerked upwards, twisting to his right and aiming for the heart cavity. Blood spurted over his arm. The man groaned, went limp.

Swan let go the haft and let him fall. His adjusted eyes could see him better now; not as a man but as a shape, not even the shape of a man but that of a collection of old clothes.

I should have taken the risk of a shot, he thought. But he'd reacted instead. It was good to react and succeed but better to have a plan. He bent and wiped his hand on the forked part of the old clothes, then drew his *pistola*, cocking both barrels as he did so. He started moving forwards. Now he had a plan of sorts.

He stopped. It was a plan that would almost certainly get him killed. Tarr knew this house like the back of his hand. Better, probably. He could be anywhere. But Swan could not wait until daylight. The watchers on the Iron Gates could start back then. And going around in the dark with a lamp in one hand and a gun in the other would be plain suicide.

Suddenly he knew exactly what to do. He retraced his steps, almost stumbling over the corpse, and then, when he was back in the room that he had first entered, he uncocked and reholstered the *pistola* and took out his lucifers.

He struck one. It flared against the dark, almost blinding him for a second. Then he saw what he wanted.

A lamp.

The first match burnt out before he'd time to light the wick but by then he held the lamp in his hand. He moved it gently near his ear. The coal-oil inside swilled noisily in the silent dark.

The second lucifer lit it and he saw the room: quite empty. There was another door. He went to

150

it, holding the lamp, opened it, found himself in a long back hallway. The open door was before him. He went outside, walked back to the window he'd entered by. He unscrewed the oil-cap, gave the room a valedictory glance and tossed the lamp inside.

He didn't stay to see the effect. He knew it all too well.

It takes time for a house to burn, even a wooden one. Tarr could get out at the back easily enough.

But he wouldn't. He would be too angry. He'd killed for this house, this valley. More than that, it had been his one chance to be somebody, not just a buckaroo or hired gun but *Mr* Tarr. The Man.

And now it was all gone. He had no men left. Those at the Iron Gates would see the flames but they wouldn't come back to help. They'd ride off, and Flynn had no time for losers, any more than Tarr had himself.

No, Tarr would want payback. And Swan himself was the only payback available.

Swan waited in the shadows of the barn. He doubted Tarr would even consider shooting him from a window with a long gun but you could never be sure. All the same, the rage would be too raw. He'd want it close and personal.

He did. Tarr came out on to the veranda, back-lit by the flames. Even at this distance Swan could see his face flushed, his eyes mad and wide.

'Swan! Where are you, you bastard?'

Swan stepped out of the shadows.

Tarr saw him.

'Why?'

Swan didn't answer. Silence would fuel Tarr's rage better than any insult. He just started walking towards him, drawing and cocking the *pistola* as he did so.

'I'll get it back! I'll get it back!' Tarr shouted, drawing his Colt. 'But first I'll kill you.'

Silence.

Tarr started down the veranda steps. They were forty yards apart in the firelit darkness.

Tarr fired first but Swan didn't even hear the bullet pass. He wasn't surprised. At that range an aimed shot would miss half the time and Tarr was too enraged to aim properly.

He fired again with no better result.

Then he was twenty yards off and the third bullet plucked at his sleeve. Swan kept walking.

He could see Tarr's features almost clearly now and could read his expression all too well: pride, anger, grief and a veritable lust for killing.

Swan dropped to his knee and raised the *pistola*. Tarr kept coming on, firing as he did so. The fourth bullet thudded into the dark earth only a foot away from Swan's knee.

Ten yards.

Swan pulled both triggers simultaneously. The gun bucked in his hand but his eyes were on Tarr.

The hail of buckshot stopped him in mid-stride, turning him instantly into a bloody wreck. The Colt flew from his hand and for a second he seemed to be suspended there, one arm raised, the fire behind him and a scream rising and dying in his shredded throat. Then he fell back.

Swan stood up, walked over to the fallen man. He wasn't quite dead but it was only a matter of time. The sawn-off had wrought terrible damage.

'Please ...' Tarr said, except it was hard to be sure. There was blood in his throat, blood bubbling huge on his lips.

Swan looked at the empty *pistola* in his hand, wondering at his own folly in using a gun with so limited a range. He could have taken him with the Colt at thirty yards. As it was, he'd nearly been shot himself.

He tossed the empty *pistola* on the veranda, ready to draw his pistol to administer the coup de grâce but it wasn't needed. Tarr was dead.

Swan turned from the corpse and the blazing house and looked back to where he had tethered his horse.

EPILOGUE

Emma was staying with the Lindstroms at their ranch house to the south of town. Swan had kept away for a day; he hadn't got back into town until well after noon the day before and he'd had business with Cummings. Besides, something had told him not to go to her with the blood quite so fresh on his hands.

She met him in the Lindstroms' tiny parlour: a plethora of pictures, overstuffed chairs and ornament-cluttered shelves. She wore the same black dress she had had on at the funeral: borrowed then and borrowed now, for her clothes had gone with her house. The thought of talking to her in this place, over the teacups, was suddenly oppressive.

'Let's go out and walk.'

She nodded and they duly did so. She said very little. Finally they came to a rise in the land where the trees had been cut for the ranch house. The abandoned stumps gave the impression of a tiny amphitheatre. They sat there, close but not too close.

'You've heard the news, of course.'

She nodded. 'You're quite the town's hero.'

But not necessarily hers. 'Did Cameron tell you?'

'Yes.'

'And?'

She looked away. 'What do you want? I don't believe it and yet ...'

She was thinking of her father. He said: 'That's a might have been that never was.' He paused, then: 'It's now that matters.'

She said nothing.

'Do you blame me?'

'No.'

'So the slate's clean.'

'How can it be?' she asked, her voice a little high now.

'Because it is.'

She was silent for a moment, then: 'I hate killing.'

'You almost begged me to kill Tarr for you.'

'And now he's dead.'

'I refused you then. You're under no obligation.'

She hesitated, then looked up at him, her eyes blazing. 'Have you cut the fifth notch on your gun?'

For answer he reached across his body and drew it, handing it to her.

'There are still just four,' she said.

'There'll never be a fifth,' Swan said.

'What do you mean?' She put the gun on the intervening tree stump.

'It was over when I knew. I didn't stay with killing in mind. You know why I did.'

She shook her head. 'It'd never work. There's too much to remind us ...'

'So we leave.'

She shook her head. Then, as if just remembering, she reached into the voluminous sleeve of the old-fashioned and high-cut dress and brought forth two folded sheets of paper. 'These are for you. I've read the witness statement as you'll see. The other's a private note.'

One sheet had 'Statement' written on the outside. He opened it up and read. It was short and to the point. It said the sheriff had conspired with Flynn and Tarr to turn over the valley and given him, Cameron, orders to turn a blind eye. It was witnessed by Emma and dated. The other fold of paper was plain on the outside. He opened it up and read it in turn.

Swan,
    Let the girl keep the statement for safety and threaten the sheriff with it at need (though I doubt you'll be troubled). How good the statement would be in court, I don't know, but if you made it public he'd never get another vote in these parts.
                                    Cameron.

    PS: I might as well be a spy in good causes as well as bad. We talked a lot on the way back. She was very fearful for you. Don't take no for an answer.
                                            C.

'You might as well read it,' Swan said, handing it to her.

There could be no doubt she hadn't read it before. She blushed startlingly. Finally she looked up at him, her eyes huge.

'I wasn't going to,' Swan said softly.

And then she wept. After a moment he moved up to her, put his arm round her. She grasped him, burying her face against him. Swan said nothing. What could he say? That he was glad her father had died before he came here? That was a subject to be buried deep if they were to have a chance together. And his good news, that Cummings, acting for the town, had been persuaded to buy the ranch for 5,000 dollars and that a bank-draft to that amount would be waiting in Railhead to be had for a quit-claim. That could keep. Especially as he'd got the remarkably good price by threatening to sell to Flynn otherwise. Or that his savings as a marshal and bounty hunter would match and overmatch the amount so they could afford a decent spread in California with a place there for her Mexican retainers?

That too could wait, especially as she might think of it as blood money. It was, in a way.

She pulled herself together, then: 'Have you got a knife?'

He handed her his clean knife which she opened. Then, taking the gun from the stump, she scraped a thin line through the four notches completing the five tally-fashion.

159

'Tarr killed my brother,' she said. 'That's for him.' She handed him the gun back. After a moment he reholstered it.

Somehow that, more than the weeping in his arms, sealed the peace between them. The Methodist minister in Railhead would merely make it all legal.